P.S. Goodbye

RESTORING HERITAGE - 0.5

P.S. Goodbye

TARI FARIS

P.S. Goodbye
Restoring Heritage Series
ISBN: 9781693826047

To my favorite veteran, my dad.

You always encouraged me
to reach for the stars and
made me believe I could touch them.

I love you!

one

Failing to plan was the same as planning to fail, and Caroline Williams refused to be a failure—even a failure at having the perfect engagement. She glanced at her phone then, put it in her pocket. Fifteen minutes late. At this rate, they'd miss the sunset over Lake Michigan.

He'd probably hit traffic. Maybe she shouldn't have insisted they meet on the beach, but it was the four-year anniversary of their first date—which had been right here. There wasn't a better place to get engaged—or a better day for it to happen.

The small waves trimmed in gold from the setting sun began to build and swell farther up the beach. The heavy clouds in the distance lined with orange and pink telegrammed the approaching September storm. Ludington, Michigan, was magical at sunset, and she wasn't the only one to think so. Other couples strolled the beach, hands clasped, fingers entwined. Love was in the air.

All she needed to make this perfect was Mason. He was probably picking up the ring. They had picked it out together over a month ago, but Mason always put things off until the last minute. Not his best quality but since he got an A in every other area of her list, he was perfect. Or practically.

Caroline slipped off her sandals and let the sand slide between her toes. What was taking him so long? A mist floated down from gray clouds above. It wasn't so much that she'd cancel her plans—just enough to add frizz to her carefully straightened hair. So, it was almost perfect. Most of the people on the beach began gathering their belongings and rushing to their cars. But they weren't waiting for the perfect moment.

"Caroline." Mason waved as he hurried toward her across the sand. His blond hair flopped in his eyes as he ran, but at least he hadn't worn that ridiculous man bun today. He greeted her with a quick hug and dropped a kiss on her cheek. His full—if not a bit overwhelming—scent of aftershave surrounded her. "Sorry I'm late."

"It's fine. Plenty of time." She angled so he was standing uphill slightly. They were almost the same height, and his shoulders lined up with hers within an inch. She'd always thought she wanted a man who made her feel small. But she'd been wrong. He was her match. She just didn't want to feel bigger than him right now.

He cleared his throat and shoved his right hand into his pocket. She'd hoped for a bit more prelude, but he was right—if they wanted to catch the sunset—the time for a proposal was now.

He scanned the shore. "Want to walk?"

"What?" Caroline glanced toward the water and then back at him. "The sun will be fully set in a few minutes."

"Right." With one hand still in his pocket, he used his free hand to brush his shaggy blond hair from his forehead. His brown eyes flicked from her, to the sand, and back to her. "Caroline."

This was it.

"I think we should see other people."

"Excuse me—what?"

Mason fidgeted with the collar of his designer jacket. "I don't think this is working."

"You're . . . breaking up with me? Here? Now?" Sure, she raised her voice in public, but—really? "After four years? On our anniversary?"

Mason glanced around and smiled at a couple walking by before shoving his other hand into his pocket and focusing back on her. "Why do you want to marry me?"

"Where's this coming from?" Her voice cracked.

He shoved his hands deeper into his pockets. "Just answer the question."

"It's the *plan*!" Caroline folded her arms in front of her chest and held them tight. "The plan we've had for three years. We graduated from college. You finished grad school. You spent a year in China. And now you have your dream job in Grand Rapids. It's time."

"I'm not sure I'm ready for marriage." He shrugged and kicked the sand with the toe of his shoe. "I thought I would be. But there's still so much I want to do."

She stared at him, trying to comprehend his words. "We can do things *together*."

"Do you even love me? Did you even miss me while I was in China?" His eyebrows wrinkled his forehead as if to punctuate his words.

"Of course I love you. And you love me." Didn't he?

"I do." He turned away, then focused back on her. "But not enough. I mean, I missed my dog as much as I missed you. Something is wrong with that."

Did he just compare his love for her to that of his labradoodle? He'd lost his mind.

Caroline was a problem solver and she could solve this . . . this confusion. "Okay, okay. I understand you aren't ready for marriage—cold feet or whatever—but it doesn't mean we have to break up. Why don't we head over to your apartment? I think I left my grandmother's necklace there, anyway. We can talk this through calmly. Make a pro-con list."

"This isn't going to change with a list." He lowered his voice and took another step toward her. "I don't yearn for you and you don't yearn for me. Maybe we did at one point. But now? We're together because it's comfortable—it's the *plan*."

She bit her lip to keep from screaming. The coppery taste of blood filled her mouth as her hands shook with adrenaline.

Caroline glanced at the crowd they'd gathered. She was better than this. She was a life coach. She'd helped a friend through a breakup recently, and there were rules.

Rule number one—No begging.

She snatched the bracelet he'd given her from her wrist and held it out. "Consider us broken up."

He lifted the bracelet from her hand. "This is the right decision and you know it. At least you should."

Caroline slipped her shoes back on and marched through the sand, leaving him alone on the beach. He didn't call her back. He didn't even protest.

The mist grew to a steady rain, and Caroline rushed toward her Ford Focus. Yanking open the door, she got in and slammed it. They didn't yearn for each other? What did that even mean? Yearning for someone sounded . . . torturous. Why would she want someone to have that kind of power over her? She'd seen how that power had destroyed her mom. She'd never let that be her.

No, a lasting marriage was built on compatibility and determination. She'd made The List to make sure they were compatible, and they'd both been determined to make it work. Until today, that was.

Music came to life with her engine, and an unwelcome twang filled the air. Country music. Mason's CD.

Rule number two—No reminiscing.

She ejected the CD and flung it to the back seat. Too bad if it got a few scratches before she returned it. If she returned it.

She flipped the radio on. "It Must Have Been Love" filled the car. She jabbed the power button with her finger. Music was overrated.

The rain pelted her windshield in a heavy torrent that blurred her vision even with the wipers on high. Twenty miles after merging onto US-31 South, Caroline passed the weathered wooden sign that welcomed her home to Heritage.

Now what?

She couldn't go to the farmhouse. Her twin sister, Leah, was out tonight, so it'd be Caroline and a bedroom cluttered with photos of Mason.

No thank you.

Rule number three—No wallowing.

She couldn't avoid her house forever, but tonight, she needed to clear her head. She needed someplace easy and safe, with someone who didn't know that tonight should have been her engagement. Her friends would commiserate and feed her ice cream, but they'd also want to talk about it. Right now, she wanted simple.

Her cousin Nate had just moved to Heritage fresh out of seminary to be the new pastor. And since the guy had lived in town less than a week, she'd bet he didn't have Friday night plans. She'd probably find him watching baseball on his big screen, unpacking, or preparing for Sunday.

She took the Heritage exit and made her way to her cousin's two-story Victorian and parked in the driveway. The parsonage was a bit large for a bachelor, but maybe it'd get her cousin starting to think about a family. Almost every window in the place was lit up. Did the guy not know how to turn a light off?

The echo of the rain on her roof declared that it was still mid-downpour and waiting it out might take awhile.

Whipping her door open, Caroline dashed toward the house. She jumped over a puddle at the bottom of the porch, raced up the three steps, and offered a courteous two knocks before opening the door. "Hello?"

An announcer prattling on about curve balls from one of the other rooms was the only response. Predictable.

After shaking off the rain, she shed her coat and sandals in the mudroom. The previous pastor's wife had an amazing sense of style, and Caroline had no desire to spot the dark wood floors. Her reflection in the window of the door testified to the damage the rain had done on her hair. She wiped the wet mop off her forehead, as well as the black smudges from under her eyes.

Her long auburn hair had started to form little ringlets by her face, and it'd only be a matter of moments before she'd be in full Raggedy Ann mode. At least it was only Nate. She stepped around an unopened moving box and opened the fridge as her stomach growled. The church had a steady stream of casseroles arriving all week.

"Stealing my food?"

Caroline bumped her head on the freezer door. "Ouch."

"Didn't mean to startle you." Nate leaned against the counter, crossing one foot over the other. His dark hair flopped into his eyes. The guy needed a haircut and a shave.

"I'm not stealing your food. I'm sharing it." Caroline rubbed at the small bump on the top of her head. "Have you eaten yet?"

"No." Nate's gaze traveled from her dripping hair to her bare toes. "What happened to you? I thought you had a date."

Caroline pulled out a pan of lasagna from the fridge, slid it into the oven, and turned the temperature to three-fifty. "The rain happened. As far as the date—I don't want to talk about it."

"He bailed on you again?" He pointed to the oven. "Aren't you supposed to preheat that or something?"

"It's a glass pan. Better to let it heat up with the oven." She shot a glare at her cousin. "As far as the date, I said I don't want to talk about it."

Nate pushed away from the counter and took a seat at the table. "You need to wake up and realize you can do better than Mason Peterson."

Caroline pulled out two glasses molded like old-fashioned Coke bottles from the cupboard. "Mason just got a job as the worship leader at his church. He wants to be a Bible translator for Wycliffe. Mason is—"

"All about Mason." Nate locked eyes with her. "You deserve better."

"The only guy I've ever liked that you didn't hate was Grant Quinn, and that was because he was your best friend. Or maybe it was because I was all of thirteen at the time and you knew I didn't stand a chance."

"He was eighteen. Your crush was more amusing than anything. When you wrote his name on your shoes . . ." Nate's laughter filled the room. "That was—"

"*Humiliating* is the word you're looking for." She set the glasses on the table with a thud. "Give me a break. It was my first crush."

Grant Quinn. The name still stirred a mountain of unwelcome feelings. What Nate didn't know was that the summer she'd been eighteen and Grant had been home on leave from the Army, they'd reconnected at a party in Canton. They had stayed up all night talking by the bonfire on the beach of a small private lake. Just talking, but still . . . the memory caused her heart to do that stupid hop thing.

It hadn't been just his looks either, which had caused many girls to whiplash over the years. He had this calm confidence about him, and he'd looked at her in a way that had made her feel . . . seen. That even though everything else in her life had been crumbling around her in those days, she wasn't alone.

She'd told him she'd write, which she did. He promised to write back. Which he didn't.

Nate had mentioned in passing a few months later that Grant had gotten back together with his high school sweetheart. That was the day she'd learned that feelings couldn't be trusted. Lists and plans could.

An expression she couldn't decipher filled Nate's face. "Speaking of Grant—"

"He's still single. You told me. Not going to happen. I don't care if my twenty-three to his twenty-eight makes sense now. Growing up has taught me that Grant isn't the type of guy I'd marry."

The type of guy who had made her feel too much, want too much. And in the end made her hurt too much. Why would anyone want to yearn for someone else? Yearning only led to heartbreak.

There was no way she'd walk that road again. Besides, Rule number four—No rebounding.

"Caroline—"

"It's true." Caroline opened the fridge again, grabbed the milk carton, and searched for the expiration date. With Nate living as a bachelor, it was worth checking. "It takes more than piercing turquoise eyes and a heart-stopping smile to make—"

"Caroline!"

"What?" Caroline turned toward Nate and froze.

Grant stood in the doorway behind Nate. His hands shoved deep in his pockets only emphasized the width of his shoulders. The blond hair that he'd worn military short now dusted the top of his collar and curled at his ears. Not to mention the scruff. The man needed a shave, and though she wasn't usually one for facial hair, scruffy looked good on him. Really good. There was a new red scar that lined his left cheek and wrapped over his eye, but instead of stealing his all-American boy look, it added a roughness that made Caroline's insides go on alert.

His blue-green eyes focused on her in that familiar, comforting way that warmed her to the core and set every nerve on edge at the same time. A smile tugged at one corner of his mouth.

"Hey, Caroline."

Oh. My.

Talk about not going according to the plan.

two

For the first time in his life, Grant had no one giving him orders, but it didn't feel as good as he had imagined it would. Grant read the words one more time before he placed his discharge papers back into his duffel bag and zipped it up. Then he shoved the bag under the edge of the bed, pulled the blankets tight, and smoothed out every last wrinkle. Not that Nate would care, but old habits died hard.

Grant pulled the tongues of his running shoes back and lined them up next to the door. With any luck they'd be dry by tomorrow's run. The thick dew had soaked them this morning. But that's what he got for running before the sun was up. Why he had thought he could outrun Caroline's words from last night was beyond him.

Growing up has taught me that Grant isn't the type of guy I'd marry.

Ouch. First Emily and now this. His ego was taking a beating these days.

Eavesdropping wasn't his style, but their voices had carried through the house. He'd tried to make an appearance before anything too personal had been shared. However, he hadn't expected *this* Caroline Williams—all grown up. Grown up rather nicely, at that.

He'd wanted to find out more about this new Caroline, but before he could think beyond a quick hello, she'd mumbled something about plans and shot out the door.

Grant grabbed the brown bottle off his dresser and dropped

three pills into his hand. At least he was down to only this. He reached for his water and swallowed his required meds before picking up his phone to scan the news. Still no updates on the terrorist attack in London last week.

Nothing reported anyway. Not long ago, he would've been in on every detail. He dropped his phone back on the dresser and paused at his reflection in the mirror. The redness in the scar had gone down, but there was still no missing the jagged line that wrapped around his left eye. He didn't mind any of his scars—just all that they'd cost him.

Grant clenched his fist, and pain traveled through his wrist up to his elbow. As if he needed another reminder of why he sat here and not fighting terrorists with the rest of his team.

No. Not his team. He didn't have a team anymore.

He made his way to the kitchen and started the coffee, letting the familiar aroma ease his mind. A new day smelled like freshly brewed coffee whether he was deployed or home. Anything familiar at this point eased the nagging tension that kept him in knots.

A door creaked down the hall just before Nate appeared around the corner, his dark hair sticking out at odd angles. He blinked at Grant.

"Sorry, did I wake you?" Grant filled a mug with coffee. "Want some?"

Nate nodded before staring outside. "It's not even six-thirty. Trouble sleeping, or are you always up this early?"

"I get up at a quarter to five to run." Grant didn't mention that he ran at that time because he needed out. He needed to see the open sky, and the old two-by-three-foot bedroom window wasn't enough after a long night.

"Four-forty-five?" Nate stared at him a moment. "So you ran five miles, showered, and—let me guess—made your bed before I got my lazy butt up?"

"Ten miles—but basically." Grant poured his friend a mug of coffee and handed it to him. "I guess civilian life is going to take some getting used to."

Nate added half-and-half to his coffee and reached for a spoon. "So, are you going to tell me why you're really here?"

Grant claimed a chair at the mahogany table. What was there to say? He'd been asking the same thing since he'd taken the exit that led to Heritage. For now, he'd stick with the facts. "Permanent limited vision in my shooting eye and reduced grip strength in my primary shooting hand, which, in the Army, is a one-way ticket out—at least from field duty. Compliments of the shrapnel." He waved his hand at the scar on his face.

"You told me about all of that over a month ago. What happened that landed you here?" Nate leaned against the doorframe and sipped his coffee in the silence.

What was there to say? Grant had always had a plan. A purpose. A direction. A place to belong where guys relied on him and he had guys to rely on. Now he had nothing. Just like after his dad died.

He'd found himself at Nate's door then too—well, Nate's parents' door. Grant had spent that summer struggling not to self-destruct before his senior year and take Nate down with him. He'd only half succeeded. But now *Pastor* Nate seemed to have life all together, and Grant had nothing. Everything had been taken from him, and no one seemed to get that.

Grant's hand tightened on the mug. He should've known Nate would push. "You could say the engagement was a shock."

"Engagement? Who's engaged?" Nate joined him at the table.

Grant tapped the side of his mug. Was it the engagement that had sent him here? Partly. At least it was something he could put words to. "Jason and Emily."

Nate's mouth dropped open. "Your Emily?"

Grant cringed. "She hasn't been my Emily for almost two years. Even then we had so many breakups in between that my mom once asked if I could get a magnet like they have for the dishwasher to flip. But instead of saying Clean or Dirty, it would say Dating or Broken Up. We probably would've married if I'd ever agreed to leave the Army."

"But you're out now."

"And she's marrying my brother." Grant rubbed the growing throb in his temple. "It's fine, really."

"If it were fine you wouldn't be here. You're always welcome—you know that. But face it, you show up at my door when your life implodes. So either this engagement isn't fine. Or there's something you aren't telling me."

There's nothing else he *could* tell him. That was the problem. He couldn't find the words for how he'd felt from the moment he'd woken up in that hospital. He just needed . . . space to breathe.

"Do you still love her?"

Love her? Right, Emily. He could talk about Emily.

Grant shifted in his chair and let his head fall back. "No. Honest. It's just . . . he's my brother. How could he do this? How could he . . . do everything he did?"

"Jason has no concept of brotherhood—never did. Think about it. You often referred to the guys in the Army as your brothers. A brother is a guy who'd give his life for you. A brother wouldn't steal your girl while you were off serving your country. He may be your stepbrother legally, but a real brother is proven by action."

He was right. Nate was more of a brother to Grant than Jason had ever been. Maybe that was why he was here—why he always came to find Nate.

Nate stood and pulled out a carton of eggs from the fridge. "Hungry?"

"Sure. Thanks."

Nate kept his back to him as he cracked the eggs and whisked them in a frying pan.

Some of the tension eased from Grant as he pushed away from the table and crossed the kitchen. He pulled the orange juice from the fridge and grabbed two glasses. This had been their routine that summer—6:00 a.m. run followed by a power breakfast of eggs and juice. Only then, they'd both been up running, lifting, pushing to be ready for their senior year on the football team. Then they'd ended up throwing away the last season in the name of teenage angst and debauchery.

"What's next for you?" Nate splashed some milk on the eggs and kept whisking.

The gray walls around Grant pressed in closer. Maybe he needed another run. "I don't know. My whole life I've had someone telling me what's next. First my dad. Then the Army. The only year

I called the shots—well, you know how that went."

"Yeah, let's try and stay out of jail this time." Nate's chuckle filled the air. "Have you prayed about it?"

It took all Grant had to keep from laughing out loud. He'd believed God was leading him once upon a time—like he'd believed in Santa Claus. But the past year had helped him grow up. After all, nothing said reality like an IED. But what else would he expect from *Pastor* Nate?

Grant stepped toward the window. The church sat across the street, straight out of a storybook with its white siding, bell tower, and steeple. A woman walking by with her dog paused to greet a man walking the opposite direction. Heritage definitely ran at a slower pace, and that slower pace just might be what he needed. "Maybe I'll look for a job around here."

"You can help me haul boxes."

Grant moved to the counter and topped off his coffee. "I was thinking of an actual job. I have a computer science degree from West Point. That should be good for something."

Nate stared at him, brow pinched. "You really think you could be happy driving a desk?"

"I was always good at math and computers. Other than that, I've got nowhere to start." Grant nodded toward the pan. "Trying to burn the eggs?"

Nate stirred the eggs, then reached for the salt. "If that's what you think you want, you should check at the WIFI on Teft Road. I heard they're looking for help with their website."

"Is that a computer store? That'd be perfect." Grant pulled a bottle of Tabasco sauce from the cupboard and handed it to Nate.

Nate stared at it, then rolled his eyes and added it to the eggs. "Not a computer store. It stands for Where I Find It. Caroline and Leah's grandpa thought it was catchy sixty years ago when he first opened the store filled with a hodgepodge of items."

"Well, that's not confusing."

"Most of the patrons are locals and think nothing of it." Nate turned off the burner and reached for two plates.

"And isn't their grandfather your grandfather?"

"I wish. Mr. Foley was awesome. But no. Their mom was a

Foley. Their deadbeat dad is my mom's brother. Anyway, Caroline mentioned they need to hire someone to help with updating their system and maybe even taking the store online. Computers aren't their strong suit." Nate grabbed a notepad from a drawer and drew a rough map of Heritage, adding a star over one building. "I'm not sure it's full time, but it'd be a place to start."

"Caroline? Work with me?" Grant picked up the scribbled map. "You guys are friends."

"Is that why she couldn't get out of here fast enough when she saw me?" Grant opened a drawer but found potholders instead of forks.

"Maybe she still blames you for turning innocent me into a hellion."

"You and I both know that wasn't exactly how it went down." He yanked another drawer open. Nope.

"True, but she sure did give you an earful." Nate laughed as he settled into one of the chairs at the table. "My cousin has never been shy about saying what she thinks."

One of the qualities Grant had found compelling about Caroline. She gave him honesty when everyone else seemed to only tell him what he wanted to hear. However, he'd always had one big problem with Caroline—she'd been too young.

"Judging by last night's disappearing act, I don't think working for her would go well." He pulled on the final drawer. Bingo.

"She sure did make a beeline for the door." Nate took one of the forks Grant held out. "Maybe you scared her off with that ugly mug of yours."

"I'm still better looking than you." He didn't care if people hated his scar. He could take any emotion people threw at him but pity. People's pity made his skin feel too small and gave him a sudden need to go for another run. He'd put in a lot of miles lately.

Crazy thing was, Caroline had taken full notice of his scar, but there'd been no head tilt, no sad eyes, and definitely no pity in her green eyes. She'd stood there in her just-snug-enough-to-be-distracting jeans and pale pink sweater. The way her cheeks warmed to the color of her sweater when she'd seen him made him wonder who Mason was and why Nate didn't feel the guy deserved her.

Grant took a mouthful of eggs then reached for more Tabasco.

"They need help and you need a job. I think you're both adult enough to get beyond the past." Nate stabbed his fork into his eggs. "After all, she said your smile was—what was that again—pretty?"

"Heart-stopping." Grant pointed at his friend. "That was before she saw the scar."

Grant's phone vibrated. He pulled it out and tapped the screen. "Hey, Mom."

"You're up. Good. How are you? Did you take your medicine today?"

He'd turned twenty-eight last month, yet his mother still had the knack for making him feel twelve. "Yes, of course . . ."

"When are you coming home? I scheduled an appointment for you with Dr. Andrews for next week."

"I don't want to see Dr. Andrews. I told you that. I'm not suffering from PTSD. No flashbacks, no sweats. Loud noises don't even make me jump. I'm good." Grant gripped the phone tighter. She was concerned because she loved him. He needed to focus on that. But sometimes her love was like a smothering hug. "I'm going to stay awhile."

"Oh." It was only one word, but she could say a whole lot with that syllable. "Is this because of the engagement?"

"No." At least it wasn't because he had feelings for Emily. In fact, when he took a good look, maybe he hadn't loved her—not enough, anyway. But that didn't make it okay that his brother stole her while Grant was deployed. Like Nate said, Jason had no concept of brotherhood.

"For how long?"

He couldn't mistake the hurt in her voice. His mother always stood by him, but right now he needed some breathing room.

"I don't know." He shook his head. "Listen, I gotta go."

"What about the appointment?" His mother's impatience had returned.

"Cancel it. I'm fine. I've got everything under control."

He did. Nothing to worry about. Nothing at all.

He ended the call and set the phone on the table, daring to meet Nate's eyes.

His friend didn't speak. Just stared at him. Stared at him like he had ten years ago when he'd walked in on Grant smoking in the barn.

"Don't look at me like that. I'm fine."

"Really?"

"You tell me. You're here with your perfect new pastor's life. I'm back at the beginning with nothing. Only this time I didn't just lose my dad—I lost who I am. Without the Army, I'm nothing."

"First of all, if you think trying to pastor a small-town church with your mistakes on display for everyone to see is perfect,"—he held out his arm and pointed to one of his five tattoos—"you're wrong. Second, you've got more and are more than you realize."

Did he? Was he? Because right now it sure didn't feel like it.

Working Saturdays should be outlawed—at least for anyone who'd gotten dumped the night before. Caroline filled up her mug with a little liquid motivation and carried it back to her office. If only she could erase the last twenty-four hours—or at the very least the memory of them. If Mason's words hadn't been humiliating enough, there had been Grant.

Her heart sank all over again with the memory.

She hadn't seen the guy for—what, five years?

She'd often imagined what it would be like if she ever ran into Grant. Only in her fantasy, Grant had gone fat and bald but she looked fabulous.

Nope.

Grant had aged well and looked . . . amazing.

And so much for her looking fabulous. Her wet curls had dripped water down her cheeks as black marks smudged her face. She really needed to invest in waterproof mascara. But with any luck, it'd be another five years before she saw him again. Surely he'd be fat and bald next time.

Caroline pulled the large envelope from the stack of mail on her desk, tore it open, and stared at the certificate with her name spelled out in a flowing black script. The ink was barely dry and she was ready to throw it in the trash. She needed to face facts—no one in the small town of Heritage wanted a life coach, certified or not. Her whole future had been planned around moving to Grand Rapids with Mason.

No Mason. No Grand Rapids. No future.

Caroline slid the certificate back into the envelope and dropped it back on the stack. If she moved to Grand Rapids now, it'd look like she was chasing him. And if she were honest with herself, she preferred the rhythm of a small town over the city. She'd been going to move there for one person—Mason.

How had her three-year plan fallen apart without her even seeing it coming?

Some life coach she'd be. At this rate, she'd be shelving random household items until she died.

Caroline marched out of her office, picked up the box of yarn that belonged in aisle three, and scanned the inventory of bins on the way. They were low on night-lights.

"Why don't you go do more work in the office? I've got this." Leah reached for the box. When Caroline didn't pass over the yarn, Leah lifted an eyebrow before turning back to the counter.

Caroline started shoving the yarn into the bin. "I'm fine. Really."

According to genetics, they were identical twins, but since Leah wore her auburn hair in chin-length curls with a few blue highlights, no one ever confused them.

Caroline needed more control than curly hair could offer, which was why she painstakingly straightened her long hair every morning. And although she admired her sister's sense of style and ability to create the most unique outfits, Caroline preferred muted colors and shopping in the L.L.Bean catalog.

But somehow Leah made her patchwork skirt work with the retro Partridge Family T-shirt today. Every time Caroline tried to branch out with her hair or clothes, she felt like a clown.

The bell above the door rang, and Caroline ducked back behind the shelves. She wasn't feeling very "customer-service-like" today.

"It's just us." Her good friend Hannah Thornton's voice was followed by the crinkling of a paper bag.

"How is she?" Olivia's voice chimed in next.

"Grumpy. Moody. All the typical post-breakup words." Leah's voice carried through the room.

Caroline shoved the last of the yarn into the bin before she joined them at the register and claimed the last available stool. "I'm fine. Besides, we didn't break up. We're taking a step back to reevaluate."

Because Mason would eventually see this as a mistake. He had to.

"Right." Hannah shot a look at Leah before turning back to Caroline and holding up a white paper bag. "I have pastries from Donny's."

Hannah spread out several napkins on the counter and pulled out a scone, two muffins, and two donuts from the bag. "Pick your poison. The scone and one of the muffins are pumpkin spice. I talked Aunt Lucy into making them again since we're now past Labor Day weekend. It might be good for tourism."

"Tourism?" Leah lifted an eyebrow at Hannah. "When was the last time you saw an out-of-towner in Heritage?"

Did a visiting war hero count? Maybe Caroline wouldn't mention running into Grant. She snatched the scone before Leah could. If ever she needed comfort food, it was today. "So much for my low-sugar resolution."

Hannah pushed her long brown hair behind her shoulders and picked up a muffin. "Good. It was a terrible resolution. Besides, enjoy the scone. It's not every day you get—"

"I was not dumped. We're—"

"Reevaluating," the three girls said at the same time.

"Well, who knows, maybe next week when I see him, he'll have changed his mind."

Hannah choked on her muffin as her hazel eyes widened. "Why, do you have a date with him next week?"

"I don't, but I think I left my grandma's necklace at his apartment when I watched a movie there last week. So, I thought it would be a good reason to stop by and then we could talk while I was there." Warmth crawled up Caroline's neck. "Besides, it's wise to remove yourself from a situation before making a big decision.

I already know he's a perfect match for me, and if he needs a bit of time before he makes that decision, then I need to respect that."

The three stared at her before Leah spoke up. "You really want to marry Mason Peterson?"

"We're perfect for each other." Caroline brushed a few stray crumbs off her lap. "He's kind, respectful of authority—"

"If you start quoting that stupid list again, I may throw the rest of this donut at you." Leah held up the pastry as if taking aim.

Lists were smart. But Caroline wasn't going to get into this debate again with Leah today. "I got my life coaching certificate in the mail."

Leah leaned on the counter, her blue nails tapping out a rhythm. "When? Why am I just hearing about this?"

"Relax, it came today." Caroline dusted the crumbs from her hands. "But a lot of good it will do me."

"You just need exposure, and clients will pour in." Olivia's pale blue eyes lit up as she tossed her blonde beach curls behind her shoulder. She picked up one of the donuts and broke off a small piece. "I can see it now. Once word gets out, there'll be a waiting list of people wanting to meet with you."

"A waiting list? In Heritage?"

Olivia stood and threw her napkin into the trash. "I have to work at the diner this morning. But, Caroline, trust me, you don't have to limit yourself to Heritage. You can do life coaching over the internet. Of course, the best life coaches have client testimonials, but you only need one great success story, and you'll be on your way."

"Online?" Caroline groaned and massaged the knot forming at the back of her neck. "I'm beginning to hate that word."

Leah pointed at Caroline. "Another reason for you to work on our website. You've always been good with computers."

"Spreadsheets and accounting. Web design is a whole different ball game. We need to hire someone." Caroline started thumbing through receipts. There were too few. "If we can figure out how to pay for it."

Leah grabbed a Sharpie and hand lettered the words Website Help Wanted across a white sheet of paper and taped it to the front door of the shop. "Maybe we can get a local high school kid looking to make a few bucks. Goodness knows that's all we can afford."

"How ironic that a store called WIFI can't get online." Hannah's voice carried over from aisle two where she stood smelling the new selection of candles.

"Hilarious." Caroline stood and took a step toward her office.

The bell over the door chimed, turning all four girls' heads.

Grant.

All six-foot-plus well-muscled inches of him.

"Grant Quinn?" Leah's mouth dropped open.

"Hey, Leah. Long time." Grant's gaze shifted from one girl to the next. "I'm here about the job."

"What makes you think we're hiring?" The words came out of Caroline with enough force that everyone stared at her.

Grant focused on her, then pointed to the sign her sister had taped up moments before. "That did."

"Oh." Her cheeks flamed. Why was she always making a fool of herself in front of this man? "Well, we can't afford to pay much, so—"

"I don't need much." He shifted from one foot to the other.

"Perfect." Leah clasped her hands together, shot a pointed look at Caroline, and then turned back to Grant. "Go down the hall to the first door on the left, and Caroline will be right with you."

As soon as Grant disappeared down the hall, Caroline stared at Leah. "Why did you tell him that?"

"The better question is, why don't you seem surprised to see him? We haven't seen him in how many years?"

Maybe Caroline should have mentioned seeing Grant last night.

Leah studied her. "We'll talk about this later. But right now you need to go hire him."

When Caroline didn't move, Leah jammed her hands on her hips and leaned closer. "We need him, Caroline. If we don't do something, this store is sunk—and you know it."

She was right. A website might be the one thing standing between them and bankruptcy. But work with Grant Quinn?

She smoothed her sweater and then walked as calmly as

possible toward the office.

"And find out if he's single." Olivia's voice echoed down the hall.

Caroline's steps paused, but she didn't look back. Oh, he was single—that much she knew. And even though there was no way she was going to date him, she was pretty sure she'd never survive watching one of her friends date him either.

She needed to figure out a way to get Grant to move on from Heritage—and fast.

three

Getting on Caroline Williams's bad side had to have been the biggest mistake he'd ever made. Grant eyed the plush chair opposite the desk with its back to the door. Not going to happen. Eight years of military training had taught him that—never leave your back open. He eased into the rickety folding metal one against the wall. It'd better be stronger than it looked.

He pulled a yellow leaf out of his shirt pocket and spun the stem between his fingers a moment before setting it in the middle of her desk. He'd picked it up on his walk here, thinking it might make a small peace offering. But by the look on Caroline's face when he'd stepped into the store, a branch full of leaves wasn't going to thaw the ice between them.

Caroline's calendar lay open on the left side of the desk, her script neat, precise, and color coded. Four pens—purple, pink, blue, and green—lined up on the right side. Color coded sticky notes ran down the left side of the computer monitor.

Not a paper out of place. No clutter. The only thing that wasn't perfect was a broken shelf on the back wall at desk level, and even that was arranged with its former contents in a neat little row on the floor.

It was the military all over again—only the rainbow version. Grant's stomach churned as if he were waiting for his commanding officer to come in and charge him with misconduct.

The window wasn't much, but he could see the sky. A bit of the tension eased from his shoulders. A lot of back offices didn't have windows.

Caroline entered the small room and lifted her chin and pushed her smooth, straight red hair behind her shoulders. He preferred the wild curls that she'd shown up with at Nate's, but he'd bet good money that this grown-up Caroline didn't let much go uncontrolled in her life. Not even her hair.

Her green eyes shifted between him and the plush seat he hadn't chosen. Instead of commenting, she sat ramrod straight in her desk chair and pulled out a blue legal pad. Her gaze stopped on the leaf.

"I know you love the changing colors of autumn." The metal chair creaked as he shifted his position. "The green ash is usually the first to turn color in the fall."

Caroline stared at the leaf but didn't touch it. "So, Mr. Quinn—"

"Mr. Quinn? Really?" He let out a laugh, but when she didn't return even a hint of a smile, he forced a straight face. "I think Grant's okay."

"If that's your wish." She scrawled his full name across the top of the paper as if she might need the reminder. As if she hadn't written it on every one of the twenty love notes smelling of perfume, the "i" in his last name dotted with a heart, that she'd left in his shoes that summer when she'd been thirteen.

Her pen hesitated over the "i" in Quinn for a moment before adding a solid dot. So, he wasn't the only one remembering.

"Do you have any references?" The chill in her gaze made the question sound more like an accusation.

"References?" She had to be kidding. He was helping her with a website, not taking care of children. "You can call Nate for a character reference. As far as skills, I have a degree and a knack for technology, but no, I haven't had a civilian job in over ten years. I've been in the Army."

She made a few notes on the legal pad. "Right. Well, I'll consider all this and—"

"Consider what? Come on, Caroline. Do you have a lot of people banging down your door willing to work for whatever you can afford? Face it. You need help and I need something to keep me busy for a while." He flashed her his best smile. That always worked in the past.

Her lips pressed into a thin line as the pen in her hand tapped against the paper at a machine-gun pace.

He reached out to steady the pen but brushed her knuckles instead. Caroline jumped, launching the pen to the floor. Talk about high-strung.

He reached for the pen as Caroline leaned down, his face nearly colliding with her head. Man, she smelled good. It wasn't the typical expensive perfume Emily had always worn. Caroline's scent was citrusy—clean.

She leaned back, showing no indication she'd been even remotely affected by his closeness as he was by hers. But judging by the way she bit the inside of her cheek, the girl was ready to let him have it. He braced himself and waited for all the words he deserved. Nothing came. She just stared at him, her pen returning to its rat-a-tat rhythm.

What had happened to the girl who said it like it was? Who didn't hold anything back?

Grant stood, and when she didn't comment, he turned toward the door. "I guess I'll see you around."

"Why just for a while?"

"Excuse me?" He turned back.

"Why do you need something to keep you busy just for a while?" Her eyes had softened as she waited for his answer, but when he didn't give one, the pen in her hand started tapping again. "This isn't a full-time job. We can't pay much. You don't live here. And the Grant I remember would never have been happy spending his days staring at a computer screen."

He leaned against the doorframe and ignored the way his lungs tightened with the question. "Things change."

"What's next for you—after this job?"

"Is that important?"

Her pen stilled. "So you don't know?"

All he wanted was an easy side job. Why the interrogation? Pain shot through his molars. He stood straighter and relaxed his jaw. "You could say that."

She tapped her index finger on her chin. "Have you ever

considered a life coach?"

"A what?"

"A life coach. Someone to help you figure out what you want out of life and how to develop smart goals to get there."

His survival instincts kept him from laughing. Barely. She had to be kidding, right? But the way her wide eyes watched him suggested she was dead serious. First his mom wanted him to see a counselor, and now this? What was it with women thinking he needed help living his life?

He shifted his weight to the other foot and pulled his phone from his pocket. "I'm confused. What does this have to do with the job?"

Her pen apparently took up twirling as its latest pastime. Her gaze darted from him to the pad and back again. "I-I'm a certified life coach. I thought it sounded like you could use one."

"You want to be my life coach?"

Her pen flipped out of her fingers and landed on the desk. "I meant you should consider one. A life coach. It could help."

"Because I'm full of problems?"

"Yes—I mean no. You say you want this job for a while, but how will that help? Deep down, don't you desire more than a temporary life fix?"

"You know what I want after a two-minute conversation?"

"I've known you longer than two minutes, Grant." The softness in her eyes nearly undid him. She'd finally let her wall down, but this wasn't a conversation he was ready to have.

Maybe he did need a real plan. Then again, plans were little more than wishful thinking for the future. And plans could be derailed by something as small as a few scraps of fast-moving metal.

He rubbed his hand across his scar and turned back toward the door. "All I was looking for was a job to buy some time. But thanks. See you around, Caroline."

He already had a mother who wouldn't keep her nose out of his business. He didn't need this woman nosing her way in, too, no matter how nicely she'd grown up.

Leah was going to have a fit when she found out Caroline hadn't hired Grant, but that was a small price to pay to keep that man out of her life. Caroline scanned her list for the day and added "Learn HTML" at the bottom and underlined it twice.

Her gaze strayed to the leaf. He'd known that she loved collecting the changing leaves. She'd never told him that, but she had *written* it in one of the many letters he'd never answered. So, he had gotten them and read them. Just not written back.

She should throw it in the trash and be done with it. Done with Grant. She reached for the leaf but found herself sliding it up by her monitor. She'd throw it away later.

Why had she even brought up life coaching? He'd just seemed so . . . lost.

You only need one great success story. Olivia's words echoed in her head. Grant would make a great success story. Shoot, women would read his testimonial to stare at his picture.

But her coaching him? No. It wouldn't work.

The phone rang and she snatched it up. "WIFI."

"Caroline? This is Mayor Jameson. I need about two dozen flashlights. Do you have those in stock?"

"No. But I can place an order—"

"Oh, that's all right. There's a company online that I can order them from, and they'll ship them to my house for free. Isn't that something?"

Caroline closed her eyes as her hand tightened on the phone. "It sure is."

The mayor ended the call, and Caroline stared at her desk. They could expand their inventory if they got online. Online. Maybe she'd made a mistake. Grant might set her on edge, but going bankrupt wouldn't be good for her sanity either.

Leah wasn't going to just pitch a fit. No, her sister was going to kill her.

Caroline pushed away from her desk and made her way to the front of the store. Grant was still there, talking to Hannah and Leah. He leaned on the front counter, drinking a cup of *their* coffee out of *her* favorite mug. The girls were all smiles and their cheeks slightly pink. Yeah, Grant had that effect on *all* women—not just her.

Leah looked up. "You didn't tell me that you saw Grant last night at Nate's."

Great. Now warmth filled *her* cheeks.

Caroline closed the distance and joined them at the counter, careful to keep her gaze away from Grant. "Hey, Leah, I saw Grant at Nate's last night."

Hannah checked her vibrating phone and headed for the door. "It's a call on one of my houses. I gotta take this outside."

"She has more than one house?" Grant looked between the sisters.

"She's a Realtor." Leah refilled Grant's coffee cup. "How long are you staying in Heritage?"

Grant paused with his mug halfway to his mouth. "It depends if I'm able to get a job here."

Leah's brow wrinkled. "You mean a job after our website?"

Grant rubbed the back of his neck. "Caroline didn't think—"

The bell above the door chimed as Ms. Johns stepped inside, her white hair haloed by the morning sun. Leah moved to help the woman.

Caroline took a half step closer to Grant. "I've changed my mind."

"Changed your mind about hiring me?" He drew a long gulp of coffee and leaned his back on the counter as if he'd be there all day.

"Yes and about being your life coach." Caroline crossed her arms tight to her body. Where was a legal pad when she needed one?

"I don't need a life coach, but I'll take the job." He set down the empty mug and pushed away from the counter.

"No deal. I'll hire you *if* you also agree to let me be your life coach."

"Any other conditions?" The ring of the antique cash register finishing Ms. Johns's sale shadowed his words.

"You leave a review—hopefully a good one—on my life coaching website I'll also hire you to create. So two website jobs, free life coaching, and a review."

The front door chimed again, announcing Ms. Johns's exit, and Leah stepped back over to them. "Now what were you saying? Caroline didn't think . . ."

Grant's gaze hopped between Caroline and Leah, then back to Caroline.

Please say yes.

"Caroline didn't think I should start until Monday. Being the weekend and all, I have a few things I need to do today." He nodded at Caroline and turned toward the door.

"Oh. Perfect. See you Monday." Leah waved and moved his dirty mug to the bin under the counter.

Grant held the door for Hannah to enter on his way out.

"Wow, just wow." Hannah joined them at the counter, staring after Grant as the door closed behind him. "How do you two know him?"

Caroline claimed her own cup of coffee in her not-so-favorite mug. "Our cousin Nate, the new pastor, grew up with him in Canton—over by Detroit. We visited them every summer. And when we lived with Nate's family one summer while our parents had . . . issues, Grant was around. A lot."

Leah tapped a sparkly fingernail on her mug. "Caroline had the biggest crush on him. She even wrote his name on the bottom of her shoes with little hearts—"

"That's enough." Caroline stirred in two creamers and a sugar.

"No, really, it was hilarious." Leah's giggle started small but grew to a full laugh. "She forgot and put her feet up on an ottoman, and everybody in the room could read her shoes, including Grant, who was sitting across from her."

"Yes." Caroline rolled her eyes and drew a sip of the hot brew. "And that'd be one of the most embarrassing moments of my life. Thanks for the reminder."

"I wonder if he remembers." Leah giggled again. "I'll have to ask him when he comes to work on the website."

"No you won't."

"Oh, Caroline—"

"I'm serious, Leah." Caroline banged her mug on the counter, sending a bit of coffee over the side. She snatched a paper towel from under the sink and wiped at the counter, her hand shaking. "You can't—"

Leah covered her hand. "Whoa, what's this about? It's more than a silly crush you had at thirteen. What aren't you telling me?"

Caroline tossed the paper towel into the trash. "Do you remember the summer after we graduated high school?"

"That was the summer I worked at Emmanuel Beach Campground and you stayed here to work in the store."

"Right." Caroline pulled the leftover muffin out of the pastry bag and set it on a napkin. She needed extra carbs to deal with today. "What I never told you was that I went to visit Nate for a long weekend and Grant was home on leave."

Leah leaned in a little closer. "And . . ."

"And we spent a lot of time together during those few days."

"And . . ." Hannah took a seat on one of the stools and leaned her elbows on the counter.

"And one night at a bonfire, Grant and I ended up talking until four in the morning."

"Just talking?" Leah and Hannah exchanged a doubtful look.

"Yes." Caroline straightened her shoulders. "Just talking. Okay, maybe we held hands. Well, he didn't really hold it, he just ran his fingers along the palm, the back—"

"That guy." Hannah dropped her phone into her purse. "That sounds . . . wow."

"It was." Caroline peeled back the paper of the muffin. "Enough *wow* that I thought it was . . . well, more than what it was. I mean, he gave me his address and asked me to write him." She'd never told anyone except their friend Janie, who'd been stuck here in Heritage with her that summer.

"Did you write? And how do I not know this?" Leah reached for a piece of muffin, but Caroline smacked her hand away.

"I did. Once a month for six months, but he never wrote back. I should have quit after the first one. I just kept hoping—"

"Why didn't you tell me?" Leah's eyes held a sense of betrayal.

"I know it wasn't love. I mean, it was only four days, but I had never felt that . . . strongly before. I was embarrassed, and it hurt to talk about it. Which is why I didn't want to hire him. And why I didn't tell you about seeing him at Nate's is because I knew I'd have to explain all this."

"And last night at Nate's was the first you've seen him since that bonfire." Hannah's eyes had gone wide.

"Yup." Caroline picked up the muffin and took a large, unladylike bite.

"Can I point out something without you throwing that at me?" Leah pointed to the muffin.

"No promises."

"I know you dated Mason a long time."

"Four years."

"Right. But in those four years, I never heard you talk about him once with this much—"

"Anger? Hurt? Frustra—"

"Passion. Feeling. Emotion. And you never described anything with Mason using the word *wow*." Leah snatched a piece of the muffin before Caroline could stop her. "I know you think you were, or are, ready to marry Mason, but I don't think it was because you love him. I think it's because you find him safe."

The bell chimed again, stealing Leah's and Hannah's attention. Caroline used the distraction to escape back to her office. She shut the door and leaned against it. She couldn't talk about this anymore.

Safe may be a sad second to love, but it was a whole lot better than heartbreak. And the last time she let herself have those types of emotions, that was exactly where it had led her.

Now she only had two days to figure out how she was going to work with Grant day in, day out, and not get her heart broken all over again.

four

Caroline had thirty minutes to become proficient in web design or—there was no *or*. This *had* to work. Grant was scheduled to start today and that wasn't an option. She dragged a photo to the top of the page. It centered on the left side. No. She dragged it again. It stayed, but the title had disappeared. And the menu bar had dropped to the bottom.

Drag and drop web design—my foot.

Caroline straightened her calendar, then lined up the colored pens. Order always made thinking clearer. And that's what she needed right now.

She *hadn't* been thinking clearly when she made the deal with Grant. Leah was right. He elicited a lot of emotions from her, and emotion wasn't a luxury she had time for right now.

Not to mention, life coaching wasn't a hands-off type of relationship. Interaction was very much required. Who cared if this would be great for her budding business—so was her sanity. And too much time with that man made her question things she didn't want to question. Like why every cell of her being craved for one more second of his attention. Because when he focused on her, she felt as if she didn't have to figure everything out on her own.

But it wasn't true. She was on her own, and she couldn't forget that.

No matter how much she wanted to believe it, she wasn't anyone special to Grant. Even if it seemed that he'd read her letters. He hadn't answered one of them. Not one.

The leaf Grant had given her stared back from her desk, accusing. She should have thrown it away. She still should.

She would.

Right now. Right—

Skype's chime announced an incoming call as Janie's name appeared on the screen. Caroline clicked the video icon, and her friend's bright smile, dark hair, and dark eyes filled the monitor.

"Janie! How are you? Are you settled? How's Paris?"

"Whoa. One question at a time! I'm great. Settled. I should be sleeping, but I have crazy jet lag, so I thought I'd check in. What's going on there?"

The image of Grant sitting across from her on Saturday flooded Caroline's mind. If anyone would understand, it would be Janie. "I have to learn web design in the next"—she glanced at the clock on the wall—"twenty-five minutes or I have to work with . . . someone. And I just can't work that close to this man."

"Because of Mason?"

Caroline cringed and glanced at the clock again—twenty-four minutes. Right, that. "Mason and I broke up. He said we weren't really in love."

"Oh, Caroline, I'm sorry." Janie's voice softened, and she leaned forward, almost as if she wanted to reach out and offer Caroline a hug.

"Really?" Caroline massaged her temple with her finger. The software manual, sitting open on the corner of her desk, stared up at her, but the instructions might as well have been in French. "I'm finding that many people didn't care for Mason much."

"Well, I'm sorry you're sad. Breakups are hard." Janie's voice tripped on the last words. "I tried my parents and Hannah, but they didn't answer. How is everyone else doing?"

Caroline sank back in her chair and really focused on Janie. Janie, who was no doubt homesick. Janie, who was still reeling from Thomas's abrupt breakup.

Caroline shut the manual and leaned toward the camera again. "By everyone, do you mean Thomas?"

Talk about a guy who needed a life coach. Not that she was itching to help Thomas after he'd broken her friend's heart. She'd ignore him completely if he wasn't Hannah's brother. Small towns could make relationships very complicated.

"I've been trying not to think about him. It's just . . . I wish . . ."

"You need to forget about him." There was no way Caroline was telling Janie that she'd seen Thomas talking with Madison Westmore the other day. "Janie, listen, you're in the city of love. Go to a café, order a coffee. Take *Pride and Prejudice* and sink into the only place where amazing men exist—fiction."

"That's a bit harsh on my gender, don't you think?" Grant's baritone voice echoed through the small office.

"Grant!" Caroline spun around and nearly knocked the day planner off her desk. "What are you doing here?"

Grant stood holding a box, leaning against her doorframe.

"What?" Janie's voice echoed from the speakers.

Caroline held up her index finger to the camera. "I'm on an international Skype call. You aren't supposed to be here for another twenty minutes."

His brows lifted. Maybe her tone had been a bit too sharp, but she hadn't learned an ounce of HTML yet.

He straightened and nodded toward the front of the store. "I'll wait out there."

"Great." Caroline turned back to Janie. "Where were we?"

"Grant? Where do I know that name? Wait! Grant Quinn? The hot friend of your cousin from that summer? Is he still hot?" Janie leaned closer to the camera.

Warmth crawled up Caroline's face as a movement by the door caught her eye. Grant stood once more in the door, a cocky grin tugging at his mouth.

"I forgot. Leah asked me to carry this back." He set the box on the chair. "Are you going to answer her?"

Why had she had the volume up so loud?

"He's fine."

"He's there, isn't he?" Janie clapped her hands as she laughed.

Grant stepped around the desk and leaned over Caroline's shoulder. "Hi."

Caroline sucked in a breath, and the sandalwood and leather scent of his cologne invaded her air supply. She gripped the arms of her chair and refused to melt into a puddle of adolescent mush. Maybe she should hold her breath.

"Ooo. You *are* cute. Marry him, Caroline."

Caroline shot her friend a look through the camera that, with any hope, would end this.

"I'd better go before I get myself into more trouble. I'm going to try my house again. Caroline, let's Skype this weekend. And tell Hannah I'll try her again tomorrow. Nice seeing you, Grant."

"You too." He returned to the other side of her desk—no, not the other side, the metal chair next to her desk—again. Like she needed him four feet closer.

Caroline forced her attention back to Janie. "Maybe someplace more private, next time."

"Sounds good. Bye." Janie's laughter carried through the speakers until the connection ended. At least Caroline had served in cheering up her friend—even if it was at the expense of her own humiliation.

Caroline needed to take her own advice and escape with coffee and a good book. But she didn't live in the moment. She lived by to-do lists, and her list said it was time to face Grant.

She scanned her desk for her trusty legal pad and a pen. "So, Mr. Quinn. About our arrangement . . ."

"Again with the Mr. Quinn? If you're going to be my life coach, shouldn't you call me by my first name?"

"Maybe we need to rethink the idea of life coaching." Caroline straightened the papers on her desk, then set to lining up the pencils.

"It was your idea. And I've decided that I like the idea."

"You do? I mean do you really think—"

"I think we have an awkward past. But we're adults. You need my help, and I need yours. This doesn't have to be difficult." He leaned forward and rested his elbows on his knees, his eyes intense. He was doing it again—looking not at her but almost into her as if he were trying to find the key to the parts she kept hidden.

She blinked and broke eye contact.

Didn't have to be difficult? He couldn't even lean over her shoulder without making breathing difficult. They couldn't make eye contact without her having to look away.

But they were both adults and, like it or not, he was right—she needed him.

"What exactly would you want me to do as your life coach?"

"You're the one who said I needed one. What do you normally do as a life coach?"

Normally do? Would now be a good time to admit he was her first client? Maybe not. "I help people discover their sweet spot, as I like to call it. I consider their passions, their personality, their dreams, then together, we make a plan. And I help them make smart goals to achieve that plan."

Hopefully, that didn't sound too much like the textbook she'd memorized it from.

When he didn't comment, she went on. "For example, my friend Janie wanted to be a pastry chef. I helped her find an internship in Paris and set the proper goal to achieve her dream."

Of course, Janie hadn't been a client, just her friend.

"So, you do this to help people find a job?"

"Not a job. I help them decide what type of job they should pursue and how. But not just for jobs. It can be for self-care, hobbies, retirement, relationships—"

"Relationships?" His left eyebrow quirked up. "Like telling your friend that she should stick to the men in books?"

"I wasn't advising her on relationships. I was trying to help a friend get over a jerk who dumped her."

There was her trusty legal pad. She pulled it from under the web design manual and reached for a pen. Notes. Notes were good. She scrawled his name in bold letters across the top of the page. "This isn't about Janie. You asked about coaching, and sometimes people need to be coached in that area too. After all, it's important to never enter any lifelong decision on a whim, even relationships. Need I remind you of the divorce rate in the country? One must consider compatibility, goals, life view—"

"Attraction?" He leaned back in the chair and folded his arms across his chest.

She refused to blush. She wasn't thirteen anymore. She stared at the paper and started tapping her pen. "Attraction is considered, but much lower on the list. Some people have better qualities than a handsome face with a nice set of shoulders."

"I thought you said my smile was heart-stopping, not handsome . . . but it's nice to know you like my shoulders too."

Caroline's eyes darted to him then back to the page again, her pen picking up double time. "Grant, if I'm going to be your coach, there needs to be some ground rules."

His hand covered hers, stopping the pen. It was an annoying habit that she'd worked hard to break, and she'd succeeded—at least she had until a certain man stepped into her life, making her feel too many things she didn't want to feel. Like now. The warmth of his hand. The rough calluses that sent a shiver down her spine.

Grant slowly pulled his hand back. "When do we start?"

If she were her own life coach, she'd tell herself to stay away from Grant, but she needed a client, and he was willing. Not only that, but there was a lostness in his eyes that she recognized. If she could help him, didn't she owe it to herself and to him to do what she could?

She'd get her life coaching business started and not lose her heart to Grant—solid two-point plan.

"I need to run invoices today, so let's start the website tomorrow. In the meantime, I've come up with a brief questionnaire for the life coaching." She handed him a packet of paper.

He thumbed through it. "Brief?"

"Yes. Now I must get back to invoices."

Grant nodded and then stepped out the door.

She'd never been thankful for invoices before, but she needed another day to get her emotions in check. Otherwise her two-point plan was doomed.

Only time would tell if Caroline's life coaching would do him any good, but the next time his mom asked, Grant could tell her he was talking to a professional. Of course, he wouldn't mention it was a life coach and not a psychologist.

Grant pushed out the door of Donny's diner. Across Second

Street, a row of dilapidated houses sat abandoned, complete with peeling paint and boarded up windows. He turned right down the sidewalk in the direction of the WIFI.

Maple trees just hinting of red on their leaves lined the sidewalk about every thirty feet. And if it weren't for all the closed businesses in town and the run-down houses, Grant might start calling the place Mayberry.

Grant crossed at the corner of Second Street and Teft Road and froze. A large brass hippo lay in the middle of the sidewalk as if guarding the path. It was about two feet tall, two and a half feet wide, seven feet long, and its belly lay against the ground as if it'd sunk into the cement.

Grant stepped around the statue and eyed the row of businesses. It had the similar look of the stores on Second Street minus the colorful canopies. That and only one of the four businesses remained open. The WIFI.

Grant peered through a stretch of dusty windows. Was that an old soda fountain? Heritage may have been a thriving town in its day, but in its current condition, it didn't have a lot to offer. Was this really where he wanted to relocate—even temporarily?

"Hey, mister, got a light?" A kid barely through puberty held a worn-out backpack in his left hand, while his right remained at an odd angle behind his back. His dilated eyes shifted as if on the watch for anyone who might know him. Chances were in this town, everyone did, except for Grant.

Grant stopped and opened his mouth to give the kid a lecture on the dangers of drugs, but something gripped him inside. It was like looking at himself in a mirror at age seventeen. He'd known he was destroying his life, but he hadn't cared. He'd wanted to escape the hand life had dealt him, and drugs and alcohol had seemed the quickest way out. Any advice to this kid would fall on deaf ears.

Grant took the kid's bag from his hand.

"Hey!" The kid scowled but didn't move. Maybe because Grant was twice his size.

Grant opened the pack and pulled out a notebook. He flipped past page after page of detailed pencil drawings of dragons before finding a blank page. He scrawled his name and number on it and shoved it back into the bag. "If you ever decide you want to quit all this, give me a call. I know a few tricks."

Grant zipped up the pack and handed it back. "Awesome drawings, by the way."

The kid stared at him.

Why had he done a crazy thing like that? The kid would trash his number as soon as he was out of sight. Grant was as bad as Caroline, offering unsolicited life advice.

But if Grant had ever needed a life coach, it had been when he was in this kid's shoes. How ironic that Caroline had been the one to make him consider a different path back then as well.

And now he was headed to her office to build a website and listen to her opinions on his life once again. Caroline had always been the type to say it like it was—at least she had been in the past.

The question was, which Caroline had he signed up for? The honest Caroline he'd known ten years ago or this new reserved Caroline. The new Caroline might not be so aggressive in digging into areas of his life he didn't want to talk about, but he couldn't help wanting to get past the wall she'd built around herself and find the girl he'd once known.

Grant bent and picked up a red maple leaf in his path. She tried to act indifferent to him, but the yellow leaf that still sat by her monitor yesterday told a different story.

When he reached the WIFI, the bell announced his entrance, but when no one appeared, he made his way back to Caroline's office. He set the red leaf next to the one he'd given her before and settled into his regular spot.

Caroline entered. "You're here."

"I'm here."

She snatched up her legal pad and held it once again like a wall between them. She was more uptight than his first drill sergeant.

Grant glanced at the floor and then back up at Caroline. "Do I really make you that uncomfortable?"

She swallowed and tapped her pen against that blasted paper again. "I know in the past—I mean I know I was—"

"Relax. We both have pieces in the past that we'd rather erase. So let's start fresh, shall we?" He extended his hand to her. "Hello.

My name is Grant Quinn. I'm here to build your website and be coached on my life."

"It's nice to meet you, Grant. My name is Caroline." She offered a quick shake before she yanked her hand back and rubbed it against her pant leg.

Man, her hand was soft. No. He couldn't go there. After all, if she couldn't handle a little flirting or shake his hand without wiping it off afterward, then any attraction he felt was a moot point. Then there had been that final letter she'd sent him—didn't come more direct than that. "Do you want me to start with your website first or get right to the life coaching?"

"Website." Caroline backed toward the door before he could blink. Even after their truce, they had a long way to go to being friends.

He nodded and sat in the chair she'd vacated. "What are you looking for in a website?"

She perched on the edge of the chair by the door. "Honestly, we don't know. We've started losing money with the growth of online buying and free shipping. It's amazing how much has changed in retail since we inherited the store three years ago. Maybe we have no business in retail. But Leah loves it, and I want to make it successful for her. But I'm not sure anything will help at this point."

Grant leaned back in the chair, lacing his hands across his middle. "What do you think the greatest strengths of the store are?"

She stared off into space. "Convenience and personal contact."

"What about orders people can place online but pick up in store? Or you could even deliver in person to locals during certain hours. Heritage is small enough it wouldn't cost much in gas. And until business picks up again, you two seem to have the time to do it. That wouldn't eat into your profits with shipping. It would also keep up the personal contact. And when people were in a hurry, it would be faster and easier than waiting for items to be shipped to them."

Her head snapped up, and for a second he got a peek of the Caroline he once knew and admired. "I love that. Who's life coaching who here?"

Grant focused back on the computer. "Not life coaching. Just a friend helping a friend."

"How long will it take you?"

"It depends on the size of your inventory, but from the look I got earlier, I guess about a week or two."

"That will be just about perfect. Then we'll set up our first life coaching session two weeks from today." She nodded and then picked up the questionnaire he'd left on her desk. "You need to complete this so I can prepare for the one-on-one meeting."

Grant glanced around the room. "One-on-one? Opposed to now?"

"I mean a question and answer time, face-to-face." The pink in her cheeks deepened.

The girl was too much fun to tease. "Face-to-face?"

"Stop that. You know what I mean." She stood and turned toward the door and then just as quickly, spun back and pointed at him. "I'm serious. If we're going to work together, we need boundaries. Ground rules."

"Okay."

She grabbed a legal pad and pen off the corner of her desk. Of course.

"Rule number one: No flirting." She pointed the pen at him before writing something across the paper.

"No flirting. Got it." He held up his hands.

She didn't look up. "Rule number two: No touching."

"No touching?" Had he been touching her? He'd definitely remember that. "Like handshakes?"

"No. Well, yes. No stopping my tapping with your hand. And absolutely no bending down to get the same pen. Or leaning over my shoulder when I'm on the computer."

It took all his strength to keep from laughing. "Are these normal problems with your clients when you life coach?"

"Only you." The words were low and mumbled as she looked away, but Grant caught them. So maybe she wasn't as unaffected by him as she wanted to let on. Not that it mattered, because crossing into enemy territory in fluorescent gear would be easier than getting past her defenses. Besides, he wasn't in the market for a relationship, and he'd bet his favorite Glock that Caroline was definitely a relationship type of girl. "Any more rules?"

"I'll let you know." She tore off the paper and handed it to him. "So there's no misunderstanding."

"What about you? Do you need a reminder to keep your hands off me?"

She stiffened as her face shifted from pink to a deep red. She leaned forward and pointed at the paper where it boldly stated no flirting.

"I'll keep it with me always." He took the paper and folded it over and over before sliding it into his wallet.

Maybe it'd take more effort than he thought not to flirt with the girl. But it wasn't intentional, and usually he wasn't a big flirt. It just felt natural with Caroline. But by her reaction, he needed to curb that natural instinct, and fast.

Caroline tapped her pencil on the questionnaire. "And please fill this out. I need it to try to help you figure out what type of job you should look for next."

"That's easy. A computer job." He pulled up the software she'd been using. It was junk.

"We still need to go through the process."

"Can't you at least ask around and see if anyone local is needing IT help?" He clicked on a browser and typed in the site he'd use to host it.

"That isn't really coaching now, is it? Besides, just because something comes easily to you doesn't mean it's your passion." It was almost as if she were trying to see inside to figure him out. Good luck with that.

"Do you want to stay local?" She made a note on a new sheet of paper.

Did he want to stay in Heritage? There wasn't much to the town, but he couldn't deny he slept better here—longer every night. Even the three voicemails from his stepbrother Jason—no doubt wanting to talk about the engagement—hadn't really set him off like he'd have thought. "I'll stick with Heritage for now."

"See, answering questions isn't so hard, is it?" She set the questionnaire in front of him. "Don't forget it this time."

He nodded and focused back on the computer as he rubbed at his scar. He'd hadn't actually forgotten it. He'd simply scanned the first few questions and left it behind.

He rubbed his hand against the pressure in his chest that had been squeezing his lungs from the moment she mentioned an interview. Sure, he could answer where he wanted to live right now, but what if she started asking questions he didn't want to answer? Or worse yet—couldn't answer?

five

Her first attempt at life coaching was crashing and burning before her eyes. Caroline tapped at her legal pad full of questions but no answers. She and Grant had been at Donny's diner for forty-five minutes, and Grant had yet to answer even one of her questions directly. She'd used the past two weeks to research and prepare for this meeting, not to mention to give herself some needed space. But all that preparation would be a waste if he didn't start talking.

She'd chosen the diner to keep it more professional. Less personal. More people around. But that only seemed to distract Grant.

Grant accepted another Coke from the waitress and leaned toward Caroline, his elbows on the table. "I know you want to find out what makes me tick and locate the perfect job—or whatever—but I'll let you off the hook. I only want a normal job. Working with computers would be a bonus."

She wasn't running a temp agency. Her job was life coaching, but how could she coach if he wouldn't let her in his life? She stared at her list of questions again. "What did you like most about your last job?"

The muscle in his jaw twitched before a less than genuine smile creased his face. "I'm good with computers. Why is that a bad thing? Did an IT worker offend you in some way?"

Caroline crossed her arms in front of her. "I'm not against you working with computers. I'm not even against you taking a desk job. But I don't think that's what you want."

"And yet it's the only thing I've asked for." He balled up a straw wrapper tighter and tighter.

"Fine, let's make a deal. I have a lead on an IT job that might work for you—for now. But you have to give me something in return."

"Such as?"

"Show me what you do to relax." This diner wasn't relaxing for him, and if she could get him to relax, then she could possibly get him to open up. It was a last-ditch effort, but she refused to fail on her first client. "Something I can do with you."

"I ride my Harley."

"I'll never get on a motorcycle. Do you know the statistics on motorcycle fatalities?"

"I've never crashed. I'll take it easy, I promise."

Then there was the whole he'd-be-the-only-thing-she'd-have-to-hold-on-to part. "Absolutely not."

"I go to the shooting range. But there isn't one close by."

Bingo.

"I know of one." Caroline slid out of the booth, the cracks in the red vinyl clawing at her skirt as she went. "I'll have to go get my car from the WIFI."

"I borrowed Nate's car today, so I'll drive. And my gun's already in the trunk." Grant tossed more than enough cash on the table and then followed her out.

He paused as they reached Nate's car parked out front. "I swear that brass thing was over by the corner."

Caroline followed his gaze twenty feet down the sidewalk to the old brass hippo. "Oh, Otis? He can be a bit surprising to newbies."

She slid into the passenger seat and shut the door. Nate kept a clean car, but it still had a lingering scent of fast food and cheap air freshener.

Grant got in and started the engine. "Otis?"

"Otis the Hippo. He's been a part of Heritage for more than seventy-five years. My grandma even remembered seeing Otis as a child. Turn left at the stop sign."

He pulled out and followed her instructions. "So guys just move him around town?"

"Nope. That thing is way heavier than it should be. Guys used to dare each other to try and lift it in high school. They'd never get it more than an inch off the ground. Once a couple of guys got it six inches off the ground but dropped it. It made an awful noise and didn't move for almost a year. The town passed a law that you can get fined if you try and lift it now."

"So, how did he move?"

"I don't know, and I don't know anyone who'll admit to knowing. Now you know the great mystery of Heritage."

"He shows up anywhere in town?"

"No. His movement is limited to the square block around the Manor." Caroline tapped her window as they passed the WIFI. "Which includes our storefront, but he has never sat right in front of our store."

Grant stopped at the stop sign and stared at the old Victorian mansion on his left. "The Manor? Fancy name for an old run-down house."

"Don't let Hannah hear you talk like that. She loves the Manor. Turn left." She placed her legal pad on her lap and clicked her pen. "Why do you like to go to the shooting range?"

"It releases stress."

"What gives you stress?"

"People asking me questions." He flipped on the radio to a classic rock station.

Caroline turned down the volume. "Anyone besides me asking you questions? Angle right on Main Street"

His hands gripped the wheel tighter. "What's your brother up to these days?"

"David is a missionary in Costa Rica, so we don't see him much." How had he shifted the conversation back to her again? "Turn right at that dirt road."

Grant slowed the car and signaled. "You sound like you don't approve."

Had that come through in her tone? She focused out the side window as the car rattled with the washboard road. "I'm fine with it. Third driveway." She pointed toward her mailbox. "I mean, I support missions, and he's doing a great work. But it was a quick decision and not enough thought went into it if you ask me. You can park here."

"Maybe you should've offered him life coaching." Grant killed the engine and reached for the door handle.

"I tried. He wouldn't listen."

"A lot of us aren't as good at spilling our guts as others. Our opening up is much more subtle." He climbed out of the car.

Was he saying that he'd already opened up to her? He hadn't answered one of her questions. And her brother, David, hadn't talked to her either.

Caroline exited the car and slammed the door. "All I know is that we could've used him here with the store. He left us. How did your family handle you leaving for the Army?"

"Good . . . in the beginning." Grant scanned the area. "So, where are we?"

"My house."

Grant's gaze flicked to her and then returned to his assessment. But this time his eyes seemed to take in more detail.

A seventy-year-old house in much need of a paint job. A yard poorly tended. The 1948 Ford truck that had rusted into the ground next to the shed. Maybe bringing him here had been a bad idea. "We have a shooting range out back."

He stared at her as if trying to piece together something, then stepped to the trunk and pulled out a bag. "Lead the way, Annie Oakley."

After retrieving her .22 rifle and a box of ammo, Caroline led him toward the back of the property. "When we moved here, my grandfather insisted that we learn gun safety. Leah and I were quite competitive, so he made us a little shooting range. It's up against a hill to capture any missed shots."

"You're full of surprises, Caroline Williams. You run a store, life coach, shoot a gun . . . Which is your favorite? I warn you though—if you say target practice, I might drop to one knee and ask you to marry me this moment."

Caroline stumbled over her feet. He was kidding. But still, why did the words make her brain short-circuit? She cleared her throat but didn't look at him. "Life coaching is my favorite—at least for clients who answer questions."

Grant laughed, and they walked the rest of the way in silence. If she were smart, she'd have made a call regarding the IT position she'd found at Kensington Fruits yesterday and never had this little meeting. It was obvious that Grant didn't want actual life coaching. He didn't want her questions, and he did *not* want her opinions.

Fifteen minutes later she'd taken down the first lineup of tin cans with her .22. Now it was Grant's turn.

Caroline leaned against her favorite birch tree while she waited for him to load his handgun. The leaves had already turned a deep gold, and her mind went back to the two leaves sitting on her desk. She didn't know if the second was from Grant, but who else could it be from? She should just throw them away, but every time she tried, something stopped her. She could not—would not—let herself be emotionally wrapped up again with Grant.

Grant adjusted his grip on his gun. He was still as a statue for a moment, then squeezed the trigger. Again. And again.

Grant's posture grew less rigid and more comfortable with every can he took down. By the time he emptied the clip, slid the safety on, and returned the gun to his side, the ever-present strain behind his eyes had melted away.

That's what Grant had been trained to do.

There had to be a use for such an amazing skill outside the military. Her mind floated to the security team run by ex-military in a novel she'd read. Did jobs like that exist in real life? Maybe that was worth looking into for Grant. After all, that seemed much more suitable for him than a desk job punching keys.

He fixed his eyes on the targets that still remained, his smile dimming slightly.

"Better than last time, but I don't have the same control in my left hand since this." He waved the guilty appendage and its scars with disgust. "Too bad that's my dominant hand."

"Is that why you left the Army?"

He stared at her and then back at the targets. "I walked away when I could no longer count on an accurate shot to protect my team. This type of shooting only means I gave the enemy time to kill me or the guy next to me. Those weren't even moving targets."

He said the words so casually that Caroline almost missed the tension returning to his stance.

Grant held his gun out to Caroline. "Your turn."

"Me?" She took a step back. "I can't shoot that."

"Are you kidding? You hit every target a minute ago."

"With a .22 long rifle. Not a 9mm handgun. With that kick, I'll hit myself in the face."

"I'll make sure you're safe. Trust me."

How could she ask him to trust her if she wasn't really willing to trust him? "Fine."

She took the gun and lifted it. It felt so weird not to brace it against her shoulder.

Grant stepped behind her. "Keep your arms straight. Don't lean back."

She held up the gun and tried to aim like he instructed. His solid chest pressed into her back. "No touching."

"I didn't move. You leaned back, so you're touching me. Don't lean back."

She took aim again, but her hands shook. His hands landed on her elbows. "Don't bend your arms."

"I can't." Her hands began to shake again.

He leaned in and wrapped his arms parallel against hers and covered each hand with his. "Now squeeze the trigger."

Caroline struggled to keep her mind from focusing on every inch of her that was touching Grant. This was definitely breaking rule number two—and possibly one—but she couldn't seem to find her voice to object again.

The contact seemed to energize every nerve. She'd hugged Mason enough when they dated to know it had never felt like this. It hadn't even felt like this when he'd kissed her.

She squeezed the trigger, resisting the pull of the gun's recoil on her arms. She shot three more rounds before Grant stepped back. She immediately missed the warmth. Stupid. Stupid. She had to keep her head in the game and her emotions out of it. She put all her focus on her targets and fired two more rounds, sending a can flying with each.

She flipped the safety on and handed the gun back. "It's a nice gun, but I still prefer my .22."

The tension had eased once again from his face. He reached up and pulled a gold birch leaf from her hair and held it out to her. "For your growing collection."

So the red leaf was definitely from him. But what did that mean? It meant she was entering dangerous waters.

"Are we done?" His eyes pulled her in. As if he wasn't asking her about shooting but something more personal.

"Yes."

He nodded, put away his weapon, and turned toward the house.

Maybe she'd research the idea of the security team, and soon. After all, having Grant around all the time was proving a solid threat to her two-point plan.

He had to pull himself together. Grant tugged at the tie Nate had lent him and paced the eight-foot cubicle at Kensington Fruits. His senses stood on high alert, and the more he tried to calm himself, the worse it seemed to get. What was wrong with him? Thomas Thornton would be back any moment and Grant had to pull himself together if he wanted to get this job. And after all Caroline had done to get him this interview, he didn't want to fail her.

Grant stretched his fingers against the unwelcome flood of energy that surged through his every nerve and tried to think of something else. Someplace else. Someplace open. He pictured shooting the day before yesterday with Caroline. The open land, the comfort of his hand gripping the gun, Caroline's red hair that had blown across his face when he'd helped her shoot.

Someone dropped something in one of the other cubicles, and the walls pulled in closer once more. He gripped the edge of the rolling chair and drew a slow, calming breath—through the nose, out the mouth. He needed to run. Far.

He hadn't had an episode like this in weeks. He could beat this.

He pinched his eyes shut and pictured the beach. The endless blue of Lake Michigan. Fresh green leaves the same shade as

Caroline's eyes. His hands relaxed their grip on the chair as her face came to mind. She'd followed through on getting him an interview, now he couldn't let her down.

"Here's that paperwork." A voice boomed into the room behind Grant.

Grant spun to face the enemy before the words even registered. Thomas's eyes widened as he retreated a step.

"Sorry." Grant swallowed against his dry throat and struggled to find enough oxygen in the room. Energy still pulsed through every cell—every nerve. Why did he think he could do computer work? Coding—no problem. Spreadsheet and HTML—a piece of cake. A cubicle with no windows and his back to the door?—not going to happen. "I've got to go."

Thomas stepped aside without comment.

Grant yanked his tie off, wadded it in his hand, and had two buttons undone by the time he reached the lobby. He pulled the blue button-up shirt off the minute he was out the door, leaving just his white undershirt. Then he marched to his Harley at the far end of the parking lot, abandoning the bold sign of Kensington Fruits behind him. He yanked his leather jacket out of his saddlebag and shoved the shirt and tie in. He couldn't go for a run in his penguin shoes, but he could ride.

His phone buzzed in his pocket, and he pulled it out. Caroline.

He hesitated, then accepted the call. "This is Grant."

"What's going on? You wanted a desk job. You wanted temporary. This was perfect."

"Can we not talk about this right now?" He switched the phone to the other ear as he slid on the jacket.

"Of course. That's your way of handling things, isn't it? Do you know you only filled out a third of the questionnaire I gave you?"

"It was long."

"It was five pages."

"Front and back."

Caroline's sigh came over the line loud and clear, and he could imagine her at her desk with that blasted legal pad in front of her—his name scratched across the top. As if she could figure him and all his problems out on a single sheet of paper.

"What happened? Why did you leave?" Her voice softened.

He opened his mouth, but nothing came out. He rubbed his hand across his scar. How did someone say that a room with no windows made him want to punch a wall without sounding crazy?

When he didn't answer, her sharp tone returned. "How can I help you if you won't be honest with me?"

"Maybe I don't need your help."

"Then why did you want me to be your life coach?"

To get his mom off his back. But he'd apparently exchanged one overly concerned female in his life for another.

He'd learned to handle his adrenaline and fears under intense combat situations when his life had depended on it. Rule number one: always maintain an escape route. "Consider yourself relieved of your duties."

Grant ended the call and slipped the phone into his pocket. He reached for his helmet and climbed onto his bike. The rev of the engine unwound some of the tension that had knotted in his shoulders over the past hour. He turned left at the light and headed west out of town. He'd found an old, straight country road a few days ago, and if ever he needed to open the throttle, it was today.

The wind blew past him, stripping away the tension with every mile. The oaks and elm trees stretched above the road, creating a tunnel of yellow, red, and orange. Shafts of light peeked through the canopy of leaves. Just like his favorite road near the ranch—where he'd loved to go horseback riding with his dad.

Grant glanced at his speed and let off the throttle. No need to become one of Caroline's statistics today. Her face flashed in his mind. The way she felt as he'd wrapped his arms around her the other day at the shooting range.

Consider yourself relieved of your duties.

How could he have talked to her like that? Sure, he was angry, but his anger really had nothing to do with her. No matter what he'd felt yesterday, wanted yesterday, one thing was certain after today—he could say goodbye to any chance of holding Caroline again.

Grant pulled into a mom-and-pop gas station. He needed a

Vernors. He pulled his phone from his pocket to check the time. Two missed calls from his mom. He dropped his kickstand and pulled off his helmet when his phone rang again.

His first instinct was to let it go to voicemail again, but she'd just keep calling. "Hey, Mom. What's up?"

"Grant. You finally answered. I wondered if you ever would."

He hadn't been avoiding his family. Okay, maybe he had a little. But he didn't really want to talk about the engagement or how he felt about it.

"Jason said he still hasn't heard from you." His mom hesitated a bit as she spoke. "There's an engagement party this weekend. Jason said he sent you an invitation."

Engagement party? Great. That must be in the pile of mail Nate had left in his room. He climbed off the bike and walked over to lean against the brick wall of the building.

"Grant? You can make it, can't you?"

"Of course." What else could he say? Anything else would bring more questions, more pity-filled looks, and more conversations he didn't want to have about counselors. If she knew about his little episode this morning, she'd be here by sundown doing her best to drag him back.

"Great." His mom's word accompanied a sigh into the phone. No doubt she feared she'd have to convince him. "I'll put you down for one—"

"Two." The word was out of his mouth before he could think better of it. But going to this shindig was bad enough. He wasn't about to show up alone—looking like he was still pining for his brother's fiancée.

"Two?" His mom's voice stuttered slightly.

"Is that a problem? I assumed I was allowed a guest."

"I didn't realize you were seeing anyone. Is it someone from around there?"

Maybe he should have thought this through before he'd answered. After all, who would he ask?

No going back now.

His mom jumped in again. "You don't have to bring someone. We just want you there with the family."

He pressed a thumb and finger into his eyes. She doubted that he'd have a date—with good reason. He didn't have one.

But one thing was for certain—he wasn't showing up at that party alone. "Put me down for two, Mom. I need to go."

"When are you coming home?" There was no mistaking the edge to her voice. "You should be here with your family . . . we can help you."

"I like it here, Mom."

"Are you still meeting with the specialist?"

Man, she was batting a thousand today with her questions. "I did talk to her today. But I really need to go. I've something I need to do."

He ended the call and slid the phone back in his pocket. He had something to do all right. Like, find a date to the engagement party or a really good excuse not to go.

six

Grant had been riding his Harley around for an hour, and he was still no closer to knowing what he was going to do. The job. The engagement party. Caroline. He slowed his bike and turned north as unanswered problems tumbled in his mind. A green sign pointed to Little Sable Point Lighthouse, and he slowed the bike to follow the arrow.

He bumped over the edge of the dunes before parking his motorcycle. He pulled his helmet off, kicked off the penguin shoes, and rolled up the cuffs of his dress pants. What he wouldn't give for a pair of shorts and his running shoes. Even with the cooling temperatures, a run on the beach would do a lot to release his energy.

Following the path between dunes, Grant passed the lighthouse and headed toward the lake. Two-foot waves tumbled against the beach and drifted back out. The sand closer to the shoreline had been wiped smooth by the water and testified that the lake's summer temperatures were gone. He stopped at the water line, letting the icy water of a bigger wave lap over his feet.

"Great place to get away, isn't it?"

Grant whipped around toward the voice, hands up, alert. A man, probably in his late fifties, sat tucked along the tall dune grass. He pushed to a stand and walked toward Grant. Shoes in hand, tie loose around his neck, and his eyes on the horizon. Grant relaxed his posture and drew a deep breath. He'd been out only a few months and he was losing all of his fine-honed instincts. He had to pull himself together.

Grant nodded and turned back to the water, keeping the guy in his periphery.

"I heard you were talking to my nephew Seth."

Seth?

"Do I know you?" He did look familiar, but Grant was usually better at remembering people than this.

"My name is George. Seth has long, greasy black hair, black hooded jacket, probably asked you for drugs or alcohol."

The kid with dragon drawings flashed in his mind. So his name was Seth? "How did you—"

"Mayor Jameson saw you talking to him and mentioned it to Lucy at the diner who mentioned it to me." He spread out his hands. "Welcome to small-town America. A new face stands out."

"I told him I knew a few tricks to quit if he was ever interested. He didn't seem interested." Grant hadn't seen the kid since that day. He hadn't really expected anything more to come of it.

"I appreciate you trying." He nodded at Grant.

Then it hit Grant. This was George Kensington. *The* Kensington of Kensington Fruits. The multi-million-dollar company that had been packaging his lunch fruit cups since he was a kid. The company where he'd just botched his interview. That's why he looked familiar. In the lobby there'd been a life-size oil painting of George Kensington himself.

George shifted his shoes to his other hand. "Nate mentioned you're just out of the Army. What unit were you in?"

Well, Nate hadn't mentioned to Grant that he even knew George Kensington. "Rangers. Then Special Forces for two years. Served three tours."

"I served in Desert Storm. Only one tour, but it was enough. How are you handling . . . everything?"

Grant opened his mouth to give the pat answer he'd become good at, but it didn't come. No doubt George would see right through it. Kensington's expression was kind but serious. Either he knew about the interview already, or the wear on Grant's soul was more obvious than he thought. Probably both.

"It's been an adjustment." The words came out in a voice that sounded unlike his own and left him gutted. Why was being honest so hard?

"Have you talked to anyone about it?"

Example A of why it was so hard. Immediately everyone wanted him to seek help. "Like a shrink?"

The man shrugged. "Counselor. VA hotline. A buddy you served with. Anyone."

Grant almost said Caroline, but he hadn't been even close to honest with her. He'd thought of calling a few of the guys from his team, but he couldn't handle hearing what they were up to right now. More accurately what he wasn't up to and would never be again.

George kept his eyes turned on the expanse of water before him. "Why did you get out?"

"Injury. I no longer qualify for field work."

"So, you enjoyed the action?"

Action? The shooting range helped him release tension, but he wouldn't say it gave him purpose. "No, not really."

George finally turned away from the water toward him. "Why did you do it?"

"For my team—I guess. Knowing it made a difference when I went out there. Being ready to take a bullet for the guy next to me, knowing he'd do it for me—it fit me, you know? There were other options to stay, but—it wasn't the same—it wasn't me."

"So, you're all about taking care of the guy next to you?"

The sky was such a deep blue that Grant struggled to find the line where it stopped and the water began. "Maybe."

"You tried to save Seth. A kid you don't even know."

"Kind of crazy, huh?"

"No. You want to keep him from walking the dangerous road he's headed down. Take the bullet for him, so to speak."

Grant stepped forward until the water fully covered his feet. "I wish I could help him. I just . . ."

"Can't do anything unless he lets you?"

"Exactly. I actually had a pipe dream once of starting a place to help kids like him. I even have a small piece of property just north of Lansing."

"What happened to that dream?"

"Money. Logistics. What do I know about starting something like that?" Grant shook away the idea.

"What did I know about running a fruit packing company? But it was my dream and look where it's gone. Besides, it's not a one-man show. Like the Army, it takes a team."

"I don't have a team anymore."

George's face remained serene as he stared at the water. "You're trying to handle life alone. But you're not alone. If you were honest with yourself, you could think of several people who want to help you—be a part of your team. Maybe not for this project—but in life. But you have to let them."

His mother's meddling. Nate's consistent friendship. Even Caroline's determination to coach him. Did they really want to be a part of his team?

Maybe, but the bigger question was, could he let them?

Hadn't he always loved Caroline's honesty? How could what he'd liked about her also be what drove him crazy about her? Maybe because honesty could look a lot like invasiveness.

George turned toward the parking lot. "I have somewhere to be, but if you ever decide that dream is worth pursuing, let me know. That's a team I just might consider joining."

George disappeared between the dunes. Was he serious? Probably not about investing in Grant's pipe dream, but maybe he was right about the team of people in his life.

The dumpster fire of an interview wasn't Caroline's fault. It wasn't the job's fault or even the impossibly small cubicles. He had a problem, and he'd been acting like a rogue warrior trying to handle it on his own. He should tell her everything. But the idea sent his heart racing once more as his legs twitched with the need to make time down the beach. Bile rose in his throat as he rubbed at the scar stretching above his eye. Maybe he couldn't go there right now, but he needed to start somewhere. Like with an apology.

Grant returned to his bike and headed toward the WIFI, but as he passed JJ's Food Mart, he saw Caroline's car in the parking lot. He turned in, parked his bike next to her car, and dropped the kickstand.

Now what? Wait by her car? That didn't seem weird at all. How was he supposed to find her while she was grocery shopping and apologize without looking like he'd followed her here? Maybe he could act like he was here to buy something and ran into her. That seemed a little less stalkerish.

He walked toward the store while running through possible conversation starters in his mind. The automatic doors opened, and Caroline stepped out, hauling three bags of groceries in her hands. When her eyes locked with his, they widened, then hardened just before one handle of a bag stretched and snapped, causing a half dozen cans to drop on the ground. Maybe he should have waited and talked to her at the WIFI.

He lunged for one of the runaway cans and then pulled the rest into his arms. Her big green eyes blinked at him.

The engagement party and the fact he still needed a plus-one stirred in his mind. Before their conversation today he might have dared to ask Caroline to be his plus-one to the engagement party—as friends, of course. But now?

As if reading his mind, Caroline stood and sent him an icy stare. "Thank you, Mr. Quinn."

Nope, no chance. Now he'd be lucky if she accepted his apology.

He followed her to her car. "Caroline, I'm sorry about . . . everything."

Her eyes softened a bit.

Maybe there was some hope. He could do the team thing. He needed to show he was trying to open up. Be vulnerable. Ask for help. He swallowed past the lump in his throat and held out a can. "I need a date."

She had to be hallucinating, but the well-muscled Grant who held her cans of soup seemed pretty real to her. Too real. And his words had caused a much too real reaction inside of her.

Caroline's gaze traveled from the bags still in her hand to Grant and back to the bags as the words *I need a date* played on repeat in her head. Maybe she'd heard wrong.

"What did you say?" The bag split and another can dropped from the bottom and hit the parking lot with a thud.

"Whoa." Grant reached for the second parking lot disaster she'd created in two minutes.

Could things get any worse?

"I didn't mean you." He ducked his head as he picked up the rolling can.

Yup, that was worse.

Caroline unlocked the passenger door of her Ford Focus, flung it open, and piled the groceries inside. The plastic grocery sacks boasted the phrase Have A Nice Day! next to the JJ's Food Mart logo. Nice day? *So not happening.*

Grant stood next to her car with the rogue groceries—as if his words from a few hours ago telling her to get out of his life had never happened. She had a few words for Grant that she'd like to say, but not one involved finding him a date.

Mayor Jameson's wife and Lucy from the diner seemed to be taking their sweet time loading their groceries into their cars. Heritage didn't get much for entertainment, but Caroline didn't feel like being the show today.

Snatching the cans from him, she tossed them in the car. They hit the seat, then tumbled to the floor mat. Shoot. Good thing she hadn't gotten the eggs, but the bread was surely a goner.

She couldn't worry about that now. Now she needed this man to go away. Caroline straightened her shoulders and lifted her chin. "When I said I help people with relationships, I meant that I help them make a list of what they're looking for in a potential spouse. I don't arrange relationships. I can recommend several online dating sites."

She stepped forward, forcing his retreat, then slammed the door and marched toward the driver's side.

"No, I don't need a match." He followed close behind. Too close. "I just need a date this weekend to an engagement party. You seem well connected and have a lot of friends, and I thought—I hoped you could help."

Caroline yanked open her door and slid in, but his hand kept her from slamming it. She looked up, ready to give him a piece of her mind, but froze. The guy looked lost—defeated.

"I'm doing this all wrong. Shoot." He stared at his feet a moment. "My stepbrother, Jason—do you remember him?"

"Yes." She never cared for the guy the few times she'd met him, but she wouldn't mention that.

"Well, he's engaged."

"Congratulations." She started the car.

He stiffened. "Thanks. I can't . . ."

His hand rubbed against the back of his neck and drew more attention to the way his wide shoulders filled out the white tee and his leather jacket. He sure had taken the Army's motto to *Be All You Can Be* seriously.

Focus. Stay angry.

Grant shifted his weight from one foot to the other and then back. "I'm not looking for a girlfriend. I just need a plus-one—a date for the party. I can't . . . I can't go to this party alone. And I don't have anyone I can ask."

Caroline opened her mouth to say no again but stopped at the vulnerability in his eyes.

He leaned toward her door as if sensing how close she was to driving off. "I'm not asking you as my life coach—I know that's over. I'm sorry I was a jerk. I'm asking you as my friend. We're still friends, right?"

Ugh—those eyes. She couldn't look at him or she'd be begging to go with him herself, and that would never do. But he was right. All past aside, he was a friend—at least he was Nate's friend—and for that alone she'd do her best to help him out.

Caroline chewed the inside of her lip and ran her fingers along the steering wheel. "This weekend, as in two days? That's pretty last minute."

"I know."

"I want to help you." Where had that come from? But the more she let the idea settle in, it was true. Something in her longed to ease the pain she saw in his eyes. His blue-green eyes that made her want to lean in.

She gripped the steering wheel like it was the only thing holding her together. She refused to be lured in. "I can make a few calls. But no promises."

"Thank you."

The flutter in her chest called her a fool, but it wasn't like she had to go with him herself.

"But first, I have to go make dinner for a woman at our church who's recovering from surgery." She pointed to the pile of groceries. "I'm making soup."

"Really? Let me help you."

"What?"

"You're taking the time to help me, let me help you. I'm not exactly a chef, but I can make the best chicken soup you've ever had."

Grant in her kitchen making dinner? Shared domestic moments were a bad idea. "No, that's—"

"I insist. I'll meet you there. I remember the way." Without waiting for her response—which she couldn't come up with anyway—Grant got back on his motorcycle and reached for his helmet.

Caroline was a terrible cook, but if Grant could keep her from offering Mrs. Mathis food poisoning, then maybe she should take him up on it. Besides, it was one meal. It would be fine.

seven

Why had Caroline ever thought that Grant shuffling around her old kitchen with her yellow plaid apron on would be fine? Oh, he'd been a gentleman, but this whole working-in-the-kitchen-and-laughing-like-a-married-couple was messing with her head and heart. Grant added a spice before tasting the soup once more. It smelled amazing, and Caroline's stomach growled loud enough for Grant to turn and look at her.

He held up a very squished loaf of French bread. "Any chance you have some Pillsbury rolls in the fridge?"

At least he'd put a wrinkled blue button up on over the fitted white tee he'd been wearing before. Just the memory sent a warmth through her cheeks. Caroline dug into the back corners of the fridge, letting the cool air wash over her. "Found some."

Grant took them and leaned over to preheat the oven. "Do you have a pan?"

"Below the stove. So, when is this date?" The date he wanted her to set him up on. The date punctuated by *I didn't mean you.* That should keep her head out of the clouds.

"This weekend."

"I know, but what day? What time?" Caroline lifted her phone from her purse and began scanning through the contacts.

"Saturday night. But we need to leave here Saturday about five in the evening, and we'd get back on Sunday."

Caroline's fingers froze. "What?"

Grant held up his hands as if to defend an attack. "It's a

midnight garden party at my mother's house in Canton. It goes from nine until just after midnight. If we drove back Saturday night, we wouldn't get home until after three in the morning. I figured we'd stay at my mom's—separate rooms of course. It's all on the up-and-up. Nate can vouch for me. I swear."

Caroline sighed and resumed scanning contacts. The number of girls she could call and ask to go on a blind date was one thing. A blind weekend getaway shrunk that list to almost none. Not to mention, who had that much time in her schedule?

Her first two tries went nowhere. Olivia had to work Saturday but seemed to genuinely regret saying no, and Leah already had plans. Hannah was her last hope. Caroline tapped her friend's number on the screen. Ten minutes later it was done. Hannah had readily agreed when Caroline had explained the situation.

No doubt Luke Johnson would be seething, but that was Hannah's problem. Then again, maybe it was time for that boy to wake up and snatch what was in front of him before he missed it.

Caroline wrote Hannah's name and number on a sticky note and peeled it off. "That'd better be one good soup, mister. Because I got you a date."

Grant slid the rolls in the oven and set the timer. "Really? Who?"

"My friend Hannah. You met her briefly the first day you stopped by."

"The super tall blonde?" He glanced over his shoulder.

"No. That's Olivia." Guys always noticed Olivia first. If Olivia wasn't so sweet, Caroline might hate her. "Hannah was the one built like a ballerina with long brown hair and the heart-shaped face. She's awesome and fun. You're sure to have a good time."

"I remember her. That'll be great." His eyes lit up, and a twinge of emotion she refused to identify pushed through her veins.

It wasn't jealousy. She couldn't be jealous. Grant wasn't a match for her—so there was no reason it should bother her.

No. Reason. At. All.

"Well, I did come through with dinner. I changed the recipe a bit, but I think you'll like it."

Caroline leaned over the pot. The savory mix of spices filling the air made her stomach rumble once more. She'd have to pull a bowl out for herself if it tasted half as good as it smelled. "What did you put in it?"

Grant leaned over her shoulder and scooped a fresh spoonful out. His sandalwood scent filled her senses, and Caroline drew a deep breath before shaking her head and trying to remember what the soup smelled like.

"It's a secret." He handed her the spoon and reached for another.

As soon as the soup was in her mouth, she almost moaned. She hadn't had soup this good since her grandmother was still alive. Caroline took a half step and leaned against the counter. "What can I do to get you to tell me your secret?"

Grant just laughed and stirred the pot again. With his focus on the soup, she let her eyes travel the length of his chin and the touch of scruff that covered it.

"It's a family recipe and . . ." Grant looked up and caught her watching him. His Adam's apple bobbed as his eyes locked with hers.

No. No. *No.* Grant was not the perfect match. Not a good match at all. Why did it feel this way? It didn't matter. Feelings couldn't be trusted.

Caroline scrambled over toward the fridge. Grant's aftershave fading with every step, thank goodness. She pulled the door open and stared at the contents. Now what? Orange juice. "Thirsty?"

"I'm good." Grant cleared his throat and followed her to the fridge. Not really helping her clear her head.

"What's this?"

"What?" Caroline peered around the door and found Grant holding her list. *The* list. Why had she put that on the fridge anyway? As a reminder to not fall for Grant, that's why.

Warmth flooded her face as she reached for it. "Nothing."

He pulled it away. "It looks like your Mason got a pretty good score."

"Yup." Caroline reached for it again with no luck.

He stared at it a long moment, then handed it back. "I'm pretty sure I'd fail that list."

Her heart jolted. "What?"

"Your husband-to-be list. Let's see." He leaned over her shoulder, peering at the list again. "I'm over six-one, I drive a motorcycle, I have a tattoo—"

"Those things aren't . . ." She took a step away, but he followed her, still scanning the list. Wait, had he said he had a tattoo?

"I love to travel—a lot."

"What?" Caroline blinked at him.

"Your list." He pointed to a line on the paper. "Someone who prefers not to travel—I like to travel."

The first two items made her sound superficial, no matter if they were true or not, but she couldn't marry someone who preferred to travel the world over his family . . . like her dad. Caroline dropped the list on the kitchen table next to the pile of bills.

Grant cleared his throat, but his voice still came out a bit rough. "And I'm not following God's plan for my life—in fact, I'm not sure I believe He has one. So, I believe that'd give me a solid D on your little test. But don't worry, at this point I'm not planning to marry either, so I technically don't qualify to take the test."

"You don't plan to marry?"

Grant pulled open the oven and checked the rolls. "Life is unpredictable as it is without throwing marriage and kids into it. Right now I'm not following any plan—that seems to be the only thing that works for a roaming single guy like me. I couldn't even follow my life coach's plan for a whole day."

"What happened at the interview?"

As if she hadn't spoken, he pulled out the rolls and set them on top of the stove. "I guess you were serious when you said that I wasn't the type of person you'd ever consider dating."

Caroline wanted to argue with him. Tell him how amazing he was. How any girl would be lucky to have him. But maybe he was right. She had a list for a reason. Maybe that list was to remind her that a future with Grant would have the same results as the past—heartbreak.

Her phone rang and she snatched it out of her purse. "Hello?"

"Caroline, I'm so sorry!" Hannah's voice burst through the line. "A client just called and wants to schedule their open house for Saturday. I would've said no, but I really need this sale."

Shoot. "I understand."

"Do you think you can find anyone else?"

She stared at Grant's back. "I'll figure it out."

Caroline ended the call and dropped her phone back into her purse. "That was Hannah. Something came up for Saturday. She can't make it."

Grant stilled. He wiped his hands on the apron, untied it, and dropped it on the table. "Well, thanks for trying. Soup's ready."

He kept a smile on his face, but the added droop to his shoulders as he reached for his leather jacket said it all. "I'll see you around."

"I'll go to the party with you."

His brows lifted. "You will?"

She would?

With that blue shirt his eyes appeared more blue than green. But it wasn't the color that made her pause, rather the hope lingering there. With that look, she'd agree to about anything. And that was exactly why this was dangerous.

Caroline nodded. "Do I need to drive? Because I am not riding on the back of your motorcycle."

"Nate said I could borrow his car so I could bring more stuff from home. Time to stop living out of a duffle." A grin tugged at his mouth as he pulled the door open. "See you Saturday."

Caroline dropped into a chair at the kitchen table as soon as the screen door smacked shut. This could prove potentially very disastrous.

Her phone beeped an incoming text. She snatched it out of her purse and froze. Mason?

MASON

Miss you.

Miss you? No communication in weeks and his first words are *Miss you*? What about *I'm sorry* or any number of things that she could think of? And why hadn't she thought about Mason in days?

Did you even miss me while I was in China? Mason's words from the breakup echoed in her mind. Had she? She remembered hating that he was so far away, but it had been for practical reasons like reduced communication and the cost of phone calls. But why were emotions so important anyway? Emotions were fickle. Facts didn't change, and the fact was that Mason was a good fit for her. The list didn't lie.

Then why did that suddenly feel like it wasn't enough?

She jabbed the delete key and tossed the phone on the table as another text came in.

MASON

Want to get coffee?

She hovered her finger over the delete key again. But stopped and sent a message back instead.

CAROLINE

Did you ever find my grandmother's necklace?

MASON

No

Three dots appeared as if he were writing more, but Caroline couldn't take it right now. She powered down her phone and threw it into her purse.

If she was wrong about the list, about Mason . . . about Grant . . . then maybe her whole approach to life was wrong. If so, what business did she even have being a life coach?

He'd thought his toughest challenge this weekend would be convincing his family he was happy—not helping Caroline dress-shop in a department store the size of his high school. Grant wiped his moist palms along his pants, then checked his watch. They were still good on time, but this had to be quick.

He joined Caroline on the escalator and sent up a silent thanks they wouldn't be shopping near the asphyxiating perfume counters they'd passed. With any luck, the headache from the fumes wouldn't last very long. "Honestly, I'm sure whatever you brought will look fine."

"Fine? Yeah, that's every girl's dream. To look *fine*." Caroline navigated a labyrinth of sweaters, turtlenecks, and scarves and stopped at a rack of long, frilly dresses. "No complaining, because this is your fault. You didn't tell me it was black tie. And you also failed to mention until we were halfway here that the bride-to-be is your ex-girlfriend."

"And that matters because . . . why exactly?"

Caroline whipped around to face him squarely. "You're not serious. The dress I brought is ten years old. It says I'm meeting your grandma—not Grant has a new girl."

A new girl?

What would it be like to really have Caroline here as his? Holding her close? His eyes dropped to her mouth.

Caroline swallowed and focused on the clothes. "I didn't mean . . ."

Grant blinked away the thought as he cleared his throat. "I'm sure whatever you brought would be great."

There. "Great" was sure to be better than "fine," right?

"No, really, it's not. Now help me look."

Grant moved the dresses around on the rack, but it was just a mash-up of shiny material and sparkles. He crossed his arms over his chest and leaned against a pillar.

Caroline lifted a dress from the rack and laid it over her arm.

Finally.

He pushed away from the pillar.

She kept looking.

He sighed and leaned against the pillar again and shoved his hands into his pockets.

"So you wanted a date because you want Emily to be jealous?" Her words came out soft as she studied another dress.

"No. My feelings for Emily are long gone. It's just . . ."

She met his gaze. "You don't want others to think you're still pining for her."

"Exactly." Or any number of labels his family had tried to pin on him since his return. "This is Jason and Emily's day. I don't want people looking at me, worrying about me. Wondering if I regret . . . everything."

"So how did . . . I mean . . . Emily and Jason?"

"Well, obviously I missed the whole thing. So, I'm not sure you should ask me."

"You had no idea?"

"Nope. They'd been seeing each other on the side for a couple months by the time she decided it was best to break up with me."

"Ouch!"

"Yeah, but I guess it would've hurt more if I'd loved her more. The lack of anger I felt was a big clue for me that maybe the relationship had been over for a while and she was just the first to admit it. Although, it would've been nice of her to admit it out loud to me first—rather than my stepbrother."

Caroline studied him, her eyes tracing the length of his scar, then turned back to the rack of gowns.

He still couldn't believe she'd agreed to be his date. He had to admit, there was a lot of tension in the kitchen when he was making the soup. But somehow it had shifted from angry tension to wanting-to-stand-closer-to-you tension.

He'd hightailed it out of there as soon as the soup was done because every moment made it harder not to think about what she'd felt like in his arms when they'd gone shooting. And her stupid list that she'd put on her fridge had been enough to pour ice on any hopes of holding her like that again—ever.

Not that he was ready to sign up to be her husband, but call it pride or his competitive nature, he hated that he'd failed the test so miserably—unlike Mason. "Why no guys over six-one?"

Caroline's hand paused, but she didn't turn. "My father was six-four, and when he was angry, he was terrifying."

Grant's hands curled into fists in his pockets. "Did he—"

"Hit me? No. He just yelled. A lot."

"So you think his yelling would've been less frightening had he been only six feet even?"

Caroline returned to searching. "I suppose if you put it that way, no. I just never wanted to marry anyone who reminded me of him."

"Do I remind you of him?"

"What? No!"

"I'm six-two."

She cast a quick glance at him, then picked up another dress and added it to the growing pile on her arm. "Okay, fine, it was a dumb thing to put on the list, but overall the list is still solid."

"And the no traveling rule? Aren't we breaking that rule right now?"

"It wasn't no traveling. I don't want to be married to a man who travels for his job. My father did, and after a while, I'm pretty sure he preferred traveling to being home. Maybe he always did. Who knows?" Caroline handed him the armful of dresses and started digging through another rack. "So where's your tattoo?"

If it weren't for the instant coloring of her cheeks or the way she seemed to look anywhere but at him, he wouldn't have thought much of the question.

But the blush made this all the more interesting. "Where do you think it is?"

Her face reddened further. "Your shoulder?"

"No."

"How long have you had it?"

"Just before I went into the Army. Same time Nate got his first one."

"Your idea or his?"

"Mine."

"You always were a great influence on Nate."

Grant shifted the dresses to his other arm. "Still blaming me for Nate's wild ways? He made his own choices, you know."

She plucked another dress from the rack and turned to face him. "Maybe I overreacted a bit that day."

Neither had to clarify what day. Caroline had wandered out to the barn and found Nate and Grant so hungover that they'd missed football tryouts. With the coach's no tolerance for drinking policy, they'd both lost a lot that day, but Nate had paid the higher price since he'd been depending on a football scholarship to pay for college. Grant would never forget the hurt and anger in Caroline's young eyes as she screamed at him, not Nate—just Grant. "You were like a possessed Raggedy Ann doll."

She smacked him in the arm. "What can I say—I thought you were perfect and then . . ."

"I failed you."

She shrugged and returned to browsing.

He walked to the other side of the rack, trying to catch her line of sight. "I'm sorry about that."

She finally looked up at him and offered a half smile. "You were young, and I've always had too high of expectations for people."

Like that list? That question probably wouldn't go over well right now.

The wall she kept between them was slipping again. He had to keep under her radar so she didn't retreat.

Caroline turned to another rack of dresses. "Nate told me that he'd been the one to buy the beer. And that you'd hidden his keys in the hay when he'd tried to go pick up some more after you'd run out."

Grant released a slight chuckle. "Wasn't the best hiding spot. We searched most of the day before we finally found them."

"I'm really not surprised that you joined the Army. You always were the hero type." She cast a quick glance at him and then rushed on to add, "I mean you're always looking out for your friends. You even looked out for me that summer."

Her words almost echoed George's, but that conversation had left him a little too raw to talk about it. "Why don't you wear your hair curly like you did back then?"

Caroline released a laugh and shook her head. "Let's see, you just compared your memory of me to a Raggedy Ann doll—a possessed one at that. Enough said."

"Only when you were screaming at me. Don't get me wrong. It looks great straight, but the other night at Nate's, it looked . . ." How was he supposed to finish that sentence? He was pretty sure all the words that came to mind might get him slapped or at the very least send her running.

She blinked at him, waiting.

"Good." His voice had lowered with the word and the way a

blush started to fill her cheeks she'd understood more than he'd wanted her to. He cleared his throat. "All I'm saying is that you should wear it like that more often."

Her mouth dropped open as she stared at him. "The night I was caught in the rain?"

"Yeah."

"No."

"I don't mean get caught in the rain." Although the wet hair look had been pretty awesome. "But you should wear it curly. Wear it that way tonight."

"No, I already have a plan for my hair."

Did she always have to have a plan for everything? "Be spontaneous for once."

She paused her searching. She didn't look up, but her brow pinched in concentration that didn't seem to be warranted by the dress in front of her.

"Caroline, I didn't—"

"Is there any chance we could make it back in time to hear Nate preach? It's his first official Sunday." Her searching resumed as she turned her back to him.

"Yeah, I'll get you back for it." With any luck, she'd taken note of his choice of "you" over "us." He'd love to support Nate, but right now—going to church was *not* going to happen.

"Great. Where's the fitting room?" She must've spotted a sign or something because she started to walk past him. She paused by his left shoulder and looked up, her face going red again. "Is the tattoo on your chest?"

"Nope."

"Oh, forget it." She lifted the pile from his arms and marched away.

Caroline was definitely too much fun to tease.

And the way she blushed . . .

Maybe he'd been wrong again. The toughest challenge of the weekend wouldn't be shopping. It wouldn't even be his family. It would be spending the evening this close to Caroline and not losing his head over her.

eight

Was she really as boring as Grant thought she was? Caroline stared at herself in the guest room's full-length mirror. She resisted the urge to smooth back one of the curls she'd left down to frame her face. Curly hair really did fit the style of the dress better, and it softened her appearance.

Whatever.

She could tell herself anything she wanted, but there was no denying that she'd done it because Grant had asked her to. That, and he'd called her *boring*. She was not boring.

Maybe he hadn't used that word, but what else did the words *Be spontaneous for once* mean? For once in your life have fun. For once let loose. For once be someone he wanted.

Maybe she did hold a bit too tightly to her lists and plans. But she could relax if she wanted to. She could even be spontaneous and fun. The shopping trip on the way here had been spontaneous.

She still couldn't stop thinking about the way his gaze had burned through her when she stepped out of the store's dressing room in this dress. The memory alone sent warmth through her center.

Caroline gave her reflection one last check over. She couldn't hide in the guest room any longer. The party was in the yard, and Grant needed to get out there. Caroline straightened her back with determination and opened the door.

Grant leaned against the opposite wall, waiting. He pushed away from the wall to greet her.

The tux his mom had gotten him wasn't a rental, that was for sure. The tailored jacket hugged his shoulders and highlighted his build. His turquoise eyes appeared almost gray in this light. "Wow, Grant, you look, uh . . ."

Why couldn't her brain finish that sentence?

"You look *uh,* too." He tugged one of her curls as a smile pulled at a corner of his lips. "Nice hair."

His voice was rougher than usual.

She squeezed her hand to keep from running it down the front of his tux. *Head in the game, girl.*

He cleared his throat, took a step back, and offered his arm. "Shall we?"

With the little extra space, she remembered how to breathe, think, walk. She took his arm and bit the inside of her cheek. Space was a must.

Caroline eyed the grand rooms and expensive furnishings as he led her through the enormous house. It was about as opposite of her grandparents' farmhouse as she could imagine.

"I'm not sure I ever saw the inside of your house."

"Mom likes to keep her parties outdoors. I'll show you around later. But right now, we're needed in the backyard."

They stepped through a set of glass double doors into something out of *Brides* magazine. Backyard? Yard indicated a casual family atmosphere. This was not casual. Thank goodness she'd insisted on buying the formal dress.

Linen tablecloths, ornate china, sparkling silverware, and crystal goblets graced the tables. The centerpiece of flowers at each table had to cost over a hundred dollars. Then there were the white lights that twinkled in the trees that all still boasted green leaves. Fall hadn't arrived in Canton yet, but the decor itself was stunning. If this was the engagement party, what was the wedding going to be like?

"Well, this isn't awkward or anything," Grant mumbled as he led her across the yard.

Awkward? Caroline tore her gaze from the finery. Half of the people watched them overtly, and the other half pretended not to. Lovely.

"They're just curious. But it'll wear off." At least, it'd better. Her mouth went dry. "Is there a punch line somewhere? Or a soda bar? I'd kill for a root beer."

He motioned his hand, and before she could ask what he was doing, a well-dressed man with a towel on his arm appeared. "Good evening, Mr. Quinn. What may I get you tonight?"

"Evening, Blackwell. A root beer for the lady and I'll take a Vernors, thank you."

The man offered a quick nod and disappeared as quickly as he'd arrived. Hired servants? Or hired for the party—who knew Grant by name? Either way, she was out of her league.

"Grant, you made it!" Caroline turned as his mother made a beeline for Grant, arms outstretched. She hadn't changed much over the years. Still tall, thin, and beautiful. Her hair did have a few more gray streaks, no doubt acquired while Grant was deployed.

"I told you I would." He hugged his mom before turning to include Caroline in the circle. "Mom, do you remember Caroline, Nate's cousin?"

Caroline extended her hand. "It's good to see—"

"Didn't you turn into a lovely thing?" Grant's mom wrapped her in a giant hug. "I was afraid that Grant had made up the whole date idea. But here you are."

Grant's jaw muscle twitched.

Caroline slid her hand into his. "Here I am."

"Not that he couldn't get any date he wanted. He's just been a little relationally aloof since . . ." His mother's eyes dashed to the couple approaching. "For a while. Anyway, now that you've arrived, we can get a family photo. You don't mind if I steal him a moment, do you, Caroline?"

"Not at all."

An arm dropped on her shoulder as an overwhelming waft of cologne hit her. "I'll keep her company."

Grant's stepcousin, Jared. *Ugh.*

A dark look filled Grant's eyes as he stared at Jared. "You're in the photo, idiot. Now get your hands off my girl."

His girl? That's what they were spinning here, but hearing it from his lips did all sorts of crazy things to her insides.

"I don't know. Us Henson boys have a way with women. At least with your women." His voice held a teasing edge, but there was a definite challenge in his eyes.

Grant's face darkened further as his eyes narrowed. Caroline jabbed Jared in the ribs with her elbow. She tried to make it simply a playful exit from his arm, but her anger had other ideas. Jared let out a grunt before he grimaced and stepped back, holding his rib. He opened his mouth to say something but stopped, nodded, and turned toward the photographer.

Grant raised his eyebrows in a way that seemed to say *I'm impressed*, just before his mother led him away. No wonder he hadn't wanted to show up alone.

"It's so cute that he brought you."

Caroline spun toward the voice. Emily's sister stood a few feet away, eying Grant—what was her name? Maggie? Marylyn? Whatever. "Are you talking to me?"

"We all had bets on whether he'd show up at all—with him still being in love with Emily and all." The woman sipped at the drink in her hand but kept her eyes on Grant. "I mean, the guy, like, ran away as soon as they got engaged."

Caroline didn't understand everything about why he'd come to Heritage, but she was pretty confident it wasn't that. "Grant isn't still in love with Emily."

"Really? That's why he brought you?" She gave Caroline a once-over. "Nate's little cousin—a safe date. I mean you're practically like a little sister to him. Everyone knows he wouldn't date you for real."

Is that why he'd asked her to set him up with a friend—because he knew that no one would take her as his date seriously? A cold sensation filled her.

She dug her nails into her palms and kept her voice even. "I'm *not* his little sister."

The girl eyed Caroline up and down again. "Of course not."

Caroline had never seen the appeal in the cat fights the girls had in school, but now? Visions of yanking the girl's head back by her styled bun and demanding her to take it back filled her mind. Probably not the type of spontaneity Grant would appreciate.

Grant said something to his mother, then turned and headed Caroline's way.

Her coming would be a waste if people thought he still saw her as his "little sister." She wasn't thirteen anymore. She'd grown up, and no matter what Grant thought, she could be spontaneous. Even if this idea was crazy and maybe even a little stupid.

Caroline squared her shoulders and lifted her chin at Emily's sister. "You may not recognize that I've grown up in the past ten years . . ." She stepped toward Grant with extra sway in her hips, casting one last glance back. "But Grant has."

Then with two final strides, she stopped in front of him, slid her fingers to the back of his neck, and pulled him to her lips. He didn't resist as much as she'd expected. In fact, he didn't resist at all. Instead, his hand landed on the small of her back and pulled her closer.

Her lips melted into his as every nerve in her body vibrated. He tasted of cinnamon and confidence. Every cell of her body ached to pull him closer—if that were even possible. She had to calm down, had to get her head back in the game. She drew in a slow breath, but when his sandalwood scent that she'd grown to love filled her, her free hand reached for his chest as if on its own.

All of her expectations and stress eased away into a turquoise haze. She no longer had a business to fix, a career to launch, or a to-do list to finish. In this moment, nothing mattered beyond Grant.

When a slight whimper escaped the back of her throat, Grant's hand closed on the material at her back as he began to deepen the kiss.

"Hel-lo. Maybe I should move to Heritage. Where's that again?" Jared's words weren't loud, but they were enough to shake them both back to the moment. Their very *public* moment.

Grant dropped his hold of her and stepped back. His eyes were a storm of unreadable emotions.

What had she done?

Maybe she should have stuck with boring.

Of all the things he'd expected of tonight, Caroline kissing him hadn't been one of them. Grant leaned back. Her eyes pleaded with him as a good share of the party openly stared. So much for hoping everyone's curiosity would die down. Even his mother blinked at him, asking her own silent questions.

Grant focused back on Caroline and entwined her fingers with his. "Didn't you say you wanted to see the inside of the house?"

Caroline nodded. Her face flushing pinker with every passing second. Grant pulled her back toward the giant double doors they'd exited through minutes before and aimed for one of the few places they'd be guaranteed a private conversation. He needed a few answers.

Her heels clicked across the dark wood floors as he led her through the house. He pushed open the door to his father's den, tugging Caroline inside with him.

The room was like a time capsule. Everything as his father had left it. An oil painting of their family when Grant had been five hung over the dark wood mantle and fireplace with half-burned logs. A sitting area with a couch and two wingback chairs sat in the middle of the room and at the other end of the room, an antique mahogany desk with engraved pens still lined up along the top. Even after ten years, it smelled like his father—a mix of mahogany and leather. Maybe it had been that his father had smelled like this room.

Grant dropped Caroline's hand and took the opportunity to get a few feet of space from her. He opened his mouth to speak, but nothing came out.

Caroline's fingers pressed in at her temples. "I'm so sorry for attacking you like that."

"I'm not complaining." Grant scratched the back of his head before shoving his hand into his pocket. "Although that might have broken rule number one. Definitely broke rule number two."

Caroline's cheeks reddened again as her gaze flicked everywhere but in his direction. "Emily's sister—"

"Melanie?"

"That's it—Melanie." She gave him the briefest glance before she focused on her hands. "Well, she was saying that you were still in love with Emily and how you'd never date me for real."

Caroline took a few steps toward him. "I know you don't want them to think you still love Emily but that you and I are really here on a date."

She reached the couch, pivoted, and started the other direction. "It was the only thing I could think of."

She twisted her fingers into knots in front of her as she changed the direction of her pacing once more. "I should have set you up with a friend. I mean, that's what you asked for."

Enough with the pacing. It was making him dizzy.

She turned again. "I didn't think about how it'd look—"

"I'm glad you didn't set me up with one of your friends. I'm glad . . ." Grant closed the distance, slid his arm around her middle, and pulled her to a stop with her back against his chest.

He'd meant the action as a playful gesture to stop her movement, but with the warmth of her pressed up against him, all playful thoughts flew from his mind. "I'm glad I'm here with you."

The final words came out low and thick. He drew a slow breath, willing his heart rate to return to a normal rhythm, but that only served to fill his senses with her citrusy-clean scent and take him back to the kiss.

She stepped out of his hold and walked a few feet away, keeping her back to him.

Grant shook his head and tried to clear his mind. He had to keep his emotions and hormones in check. This wasn't a real date. She didn't want this. She didn't want him.

"But everyone out there only sees the braces-faced thirteen-year-old who was obsessed with you and left you love notes in your shoes every time you visited Nate that summer."

He dropped onto the couch and let his laughter fill the room. "No one is going to confuse you for thirteen, Caroline."

She shot him a frustrated look. "You know what I mean."

Grant leaned forward on his elbows. "You were—"

"Obnoxious. Pathetic—"

"Honest." Grant locked eyes with her.

Caroline gripped the back of the wingback chair that she'd positioned herself behind like a shield.

Grant hated talking about that point in his life, but maybe it was time to open that door. At least a crack. "That was the summer I lost my dad. My dad, who I didn't even know was sick until it was too late to say goodbye."

"They didn't tell you?"

"It was an aggressive brain tumor. My parents thought they were helping by not telling me as I wrapped up my finals my junior year. Then I left almost immediately for football camp. My mom said they were going to tell me when I got back. He slipped into a coma the day before I returned and never woke up."

"Oh, Grant. I'm sorry."

"He died before June was over. Even later, my mom was never good at talking about it. Not even my grandparents. They kept it all locked away. But you . . . That summer you shared all your feelings in every note."

Caroline sat in the chair she'd been hiding behind and covered her face with her hands. "Don't remind me."

Grant scooted forward until his knees almost bumped hers and reached for her wrists. He pulled her hands from her face. Gentle enough for her to pull free if she wanted. "I loved it."

"What?" Caroline sat up straighter, leaving her wrists in his hands.

Grant shifted their hands to a comfortable position and trailed his thumbs across the soft skin at her wrists. "Not in a creepy way. I mean, you were thirteen and I was almost eighteen and that would've been—"

"Gross?" A slight giggle escaped with her word.

"Yes. But I loved your honesty. I actually kept the notes as a reminder that I wanted to be more like that—open, honest. Willing to lay it all out there."

She lifted an eyebrow at him. "You? Just lay it all out there?"

"I didn't say I was good at it. After all, I was raised in this house, and habits run deep. But it is who I want to be." Maybe he shouldn't have brought up the past. But he'd already cracked the door this far so might as well step fully in. After all, they had so much history between them, but it was time to lay a few pieces out there. "And I kept all your letters from the other summer too. I'm sorry I never wrote back."

Her arms stiffened in his hands.

"Why didn't you?" Her soft words barely reached him.

"You were still young. I know you were eighteen, but that *is* young and innocent. You had so much life yet to discover. And by the time I got your first letter, Emily and I were back together."

"But you didn't write once."

He'd started one at least a dozen times, only to have each one land in the trash. "I knew if I wrote one, it would turn into two and then three. And I knew after our conversation by the fire that night that there was no way I could write back and forth to you and not think about you as more than a friend should. It wouldn't have been fair to Emily."

"Oh." She pulled her hands free and stood.

"I'm sorry." He rubbed his hands together to keep from reaching for her again.

"I'm not mad." She picked at a seam of the chair. "It's just . . . I guess I've always assumed—believed—that I'd read too much into the conversation. Imagined . . . well, everything."

"You didn't." He stood, stepped closer, and waited until she looked at him again. "It was just bad timing. But now—"

He cleared his throat and broke eye contact. He had to remember that no matter how she looked at him now, Caroline had made it clear over the past week that he wasn't the guy for her. Then again, that kiss had said something entirely different. But how did he get that Caroline to come back?

Caroline picked up an old photo from the shelf next to her. "Is this you and your dad?"

"That's us."

"He looks really proud. You must have been close."

Grant pulled the photo from her hands. His reflection these days looked a lot more like his dad in the photo than the younger version of himself. Too bad he didn't feel like his dad. His dad always had a plan—a direction. He knew what he wanted and went after it.

Grant didn't have any direction right now.

He focused on Caroline's reflection in the glass. Or maybe he did, and maybe it was time to go after her.

He reached for her hand. "So, about that kiss."

She stilled but didn't look up.

"Let's go with it."

"What?" Her voice hit an unusually high pitch.

He shrugged and intertwined their fingers. "It'll keep everyone off my back. They won't question me staying in Heritage if they think we're together."

Then he leaned closer to her ear. "Besides, it doesn't feel so dishonest all of a sudden."

nine

Now what? Caroline pulled the cover up to her chin, stared at the guest room's ceiling, and wished teleportation was real. But it wasn't, and she couldn't avoid Grant much longer. It wasn't that she was angry with him.

Last night had been . . . well, amazing. They hadn't shared any more kisses like the *one*. But there had been so many little touches. On her hand. On the small of her back. Or her shoulder. Brushing her hair from her face.

And when he'd danced with her to "Sweet Caroline" while singing along in an off-key voice, she found herself laughing and relaxing in a way she hadn't in years. There'd been a reason she'd lost her heart to him at thirteen and then again at eighteen. In so many ways they just . . . fit.

Caroline pressed her cool hands against her warming cheeks. She'd never wanted last night to end. But it had. And now she had to figure out today.

Why did life have to be so complicated?

For so many years she'd forced herself to believe that her memory at eighteen had been wrong. That she'd foolishly read into his words—his behavior. But he as much admitted last night that he'd liked her too. Part of her wanted to soak in that knowledge like a giddy schoolgirl.

But the other part . . . the part that kept her glued to this bed was the realization that whatever he'd felt all those years ago—it hadn't been enough. He'd chosen someone else—something else.

Funny, he'd kept her letters as a reminder of who he wanted to be, and Caroline had kept the memory of those letters as a reminder of who *not* to be.

Don't tell a man you love him first.

Don't go after a guy who made it clear he wasn't interested.

Don't open up your heart for extreme disappointment.

He may think he wanted her now, in the moment. But moments changed. And one day Grant would wake up and realize again that she wasn't what he wanted and he should have planned better.

Only by then she'd have grown addicted to the warmth he offered, and when he ended things, it would destroy her. Just like how her dad's leaving had destroyed her mom.

Grant didn't even want to get married. He'd said as much. Which was a guy's way of saying *I like you, but don't get attached because I'm not serious about us.* Many guys said they weren't interested in marriage until they found the girl they wanted to marry. She was only a distraction for him in his out of control life. It was time to be her own life coach and tell herself not to trust these feelings for Grant.

She just had to play it cool until they got back to Heritage, and Grant would assume that everything last night from her side had been part of their act. He'd believe she wasn't really interested, and he'd forget all about her. Like last time.

Caroline sat up and pushed off the bed. She scooped up her clothes and yanked the door to her private bathroom open.

"Morning. Sleep well?" Grant stood by the sink looking in the mirror, face half-covered in shaving cream, and a razor in hand. He glanced at her in his reflection before he returned to shaving. He had a towel around his neck and a pair of well-worn jeans hanging on his hips but no shirt.

Not a private bathroom? She lifted her bundle of clothes in front of her, unable to pull her gaze from his bare shoulders. "You're in my bathroom."

That was brilliant.

"Sorry, it's a Brady Bunch bathroom." Grant pointed to the door that led to his room.

She'd seen that door the night before but assumed it was just a closet for extra towels. Good thing she hadn't opened it.

He pulled the towel from his neck and wiped away any remains of shaving cream before hanging it on a bar. "I'm almost done."

And there was his bare chest. With muscles. Defined muscles.

The Army was such a worthy cause.

Her pulse picked up speed at the memory of him holding her against that chest as they danced. At the way he'd tucked her head against his shoulder as he leaned in to whisper funny comments throughout the night. At how the breath from his words had tickled the edges of her neck, sending a current down her spine.

She pulled her eyes away from his chest to find his intense gaze watching her in the mirror.

She was not pulling off the unaffected plan.

"Found your tattoo." The pitch of her voice caused his eyebrows to stretch to his hairline. She really shouldn't be allowed to speak before coffee. Or with a shirtless man.

A smile creased his face as he lifted his arm, exposing his left side. "I didn't know you'd been searching for it."

No flirting.

Not that she could say that after they'd spent all last evening breaking rules one and two over and over.

He glanced in the mirror at the tattoo with an unreadable expression. "Ironic that the guy who can't seem to find his way has a compass rose tattoo, huh?"

Caroline blinked at him and studied the dark lines that spanned the width of his rib cage. Her mouth went dry as she tried to think of a response. She'd always seen tattoos as stupid, a waste of money. But this was amazing. She stepped closer, gripping the clothes in her hands tighter to keep from reaching for the tattoo and tracing it with her fingers.

When Grant spoke again, his voice had grown thicker. "My dad had a similar one. I got it on the one-year anniversary of his death as a reminder of the path my dad followed. The Army. His faith. I joined the Army shortly after. I guess I was just a kid trying to be like his dad."

"It's a gift to have a person in your life who points you in the right direction. It sounds like your dad was a good guy."

"He was." He put his arm down as his eyes found hers again. "So about last night—"

"Let me know when you're done." Caroline turned in a swift motion and headed for her door.

They did need to talk about everything that happened last night, but not in here. Not while they stood there sharing secrets. And not while he was half naked. She had to stay strong. Another second in here and that wasn't going to happen.

"Wait."

She stopped but didn't turn around.

He sighed, and his tone altered as if he'd changed his mind about what he was going to say. "I'd like to stop by my ranch on the way home. If that's okay."

"Ranch?" She turned her head, enough to catch him in her peripheral vision, but not enough to see him fully.

He shrugged. "That's what we call it. It's just thirty acres where we kept our horses once upon a time. Now it's an old deserted barn."

"You had horses?"

"They were my dad's and my thing when I was a kid. First, I got too busy with football, and then when my dad passed, they were all sold. But he left the property and barn in my name. I haven't been there in a long time. Thought it might be time. Are you up for that?"

"I'd like to see it." She couldn't help but want to know as much about Grant as she could, even if it made it harder to walk away in the end.

"But if you want to make it back for church, we need to leave in about thirty minutes."

"Okay. I can do that. But you need to get dressed. I mean we need to get dressed. Separately. Get clothes. On." She really had to stop talking.

He laughed as he reached for his door, and her face flamed with warmth again.

Going to the ranch was probably a mistake. But there was something about him that made her long for more. More conversations. More insight into who he really was. And more time together.

She was in so much trouble. Because all this *more* was sure to have the same result as last time.

More heartache.

Every time Grant thought he had Caroline figured out, she threw him a curveball. He glanced at her as he turned down the long dirt road that led to his property. Her eyes were fixed out the side window as she sat mute. Much the way she'd been from the minute they'd pulled out of his mother's driveway.

Memories of Caroline from the previous night filled his mind. The way they'd danced, laughed, even added a few more quick kisses for show. Each kiss had been nothing more than a peck, but by the end of the night he'd begun to crave the taste of her.

She'd relaxed, softened, and he'd thought they might actually be getting somewhere. He'd even planned to kiss her goodnight away from prying eyes. A real kiss. A kiss that would finish the one that she surprised him with at the party. But the moment they'd walked toward their rooms, she dropped his hand and raised a wall. What had he done wrong?

It probably was that blasted list. He'd thought he'd get a few items checked off in his column. Like opening up. He'd shared a lot last night with Caroline. More than he'd ever shared with anyone. But that one check didn't seem to have gotten him very far.

After all, Mason had a neat little check in every column. The guy was like a Christian Superman. Was it possible for him to hate someone he'd never met?

Admittedly, some of the items were downright ridiculous. But others couldn't be dismissed so easily. What about traveling? He loved to travel. He'd never love it more than a family, if he ever had one—but give it up totally?

Then there was the whole follow-God-wherever clause. Well, Grant had thought he'd been following God when he went into the military, and that hadn't worked out as planned.

But this was all crazy. Couldn't they simply go out and have a good time without planning what would come next? The girl wanted to have the details of the marriage and the happily-ever-after ending planned from the first date. Life didn't work that way.

Grant stopped the car in front of the old barn. The wood was a little more weathered and the weeds taller, but other than that, time had stood still. The hanging tire where he'd been working on his throwing arm still twisted in the breeze. The old dirt bike he used to ride around the property lay abandoned to the side of the barn. The half-mended fence he'd been fixing with his dad the last time they'd been here waited incomplete.

His chest tightened, and pressure built at the back of his eyes. He turned his face away from Caroline. Maybe coming here with her was a mistake.

"When's the last time you were here?"

He cleared his throat. "Before my dad got sick. Well, before they told me my dad was sick."

Caroline squeezed his arm. "Do you want me to wait here?"

"No. Let's do this." Grant climbed out of the car and approached the fence line.

He lifted a beech tree leaf that had landed on the post. The leaf was still part green, but a bit of yellow, red, and orange pushed in from one side. Almost as if the leaf had been trying to cling to the last of summer but failed.

Grant held out the leaf to Caroline. She hesitated, then took it.

He turned back to the half-mended fence and leaned on it. "We argued over this fence the last day we were here. He wanted to finish it, and I wanted to get back for a party at school. I won."

Grant pulled a long piece of grass from the ground and rolled it between his fingers. "I don't remember a thing about that party or why I wanted to go. But I do remember my dad's face just before he'd agreed—as if he wanted to tell me something."

Grant flicked the grass to the ground then reached for another. "If he'd told me—if he'd been honest with me—about everything . . . I would've stayed that day, and I would've stayed home from football camp too. I would've been there."

"I'm not saying I agree with your dad for not telling you, but maybe he did it because he wanted you to be happy and carefree as long as you could. To be a kid." Caroline leaned on the fence, their elbows brushing. "Losing your parent forces you to grow up—fast. He knew he couldn't protect you from that, but he *could* put it off as long as possible."

Grant had always seen his father not opening up about the cancer as an easy way out. He stared down at a board barely visible in the tall grass. He'd watched his dad carry the board that day. His face had been tense. Now looking back, his father had been in pain. Maybe he'd taken on the extra pain to make life easier for Grant. Some of the anger he'd shouldered for the past ten years melted away.

"Have you ever thought about fixing this place up?"

Grant stood up straighter and scanned the property. His pipe dream he'd told George Kensington about flashed in his mind. A working ranch with horses and farm duties for kids who were starting down the wrong path. He could almost see it.

But how could he help others if he couldn't even fix his own problems? "But that would take money, so that isn't really an option. I need to find a job."

"Right, job." Her eyes filled with the question he still hadn't answered—the interview.

He wanted to tell her, he did—but the words wouldn't come. He could only take so much baring of the soul in one weekend. Besides, how could he say *I can't handle not being able to see the sky* without sounding crazy? And he was pretty sure that crazy wasn't on Caroline's perfect-husband list.

"There's a small apartment in the top of the barn. Dad hired a college student to look after the horses on a day-to-day basis. Near the end we weren't even making it out every weekend." Grant stared across the land again, ignoring the guilt that tugged at him for changing subjects. "Maybe I'll fix it up someday—all of it."

"Yeah, someday." She walked a few feet away, the wind lifting her hair as disappointment filled her face.

Grant tightened his fist and kicked at the dirt. No matter how much he gave, she still wanted more—only more at arm's length, with no flirting and no touching. They were back to the beginning, and she was being his life coach again, only this time unofficially.

George's words about his team came back to him. Maybe she wasn't falling for him at all. He was falling for her, and she was just trying to help him out. A team player.

Then again, the guys on his Special Forces team didn't turn that sweet shade of pink when they walked in on him shirtless in the bathroom. And that kiss sure hadn't felt like a team player.

He shifted his weight to one foot and scanned the property, shading his eyes against the sun. In his military teams, he didn't have to deal with romance clouding things—that was for sure. "Caroline, about last night—"

"It was an act, nothing more." Her words tumbled together, tearing a little bit of Grant's heart with every word.

"Right." Grant focused on Caroline, her teeth biting at her bottom lip as she avoided his gaze. The girl was a terrible liar, but if this was how she wanted to play it, he couldn't fight it. He obviously hadn't crossed off enough of her list last night and didn't see how he ever could.

But he wasn't ready to give up yet.

"Want to show me more?"

He wanted to show her that her list was a ridiculous paper fantasy. He wanted to show her that if she'd give them a chance, they could be good—great—together. He wanted to show her that the fearless Caroline he'd known years ago was still in there.

Grant pulled out his phone and checked the time. "It took longer than I thought to get here. We'd better go if we're going to get you back in time for church."

She nodded and turned back to the car.

The heaviness in Grant's chest grew with every step. Once they returned to Heritage, they'd have no real reason to spend time together anymore.

Grant slid into the car and started the engine. "Would you consider being my life coach again?"

She turned the leaf he'd given her over in her fingers, then again. "Do you want that?"

He offered her a half smile. "I still don't have any leads, and I'm almost done with the store's website. Which reminds me, we need to get your life coaching website finished up too. I just need your content."

"I thought I gave you all that."

"No, you gave me a color scheme and design ideas. But this is representing you. What do you want to say about Caroline Williams to the world?"

Caroline picked at her fingernail. "Do you want me to look for another computer job? For when the website is done?"

He focused on the road. "Maybe you were right when you said computers weren't a good fit for me. So, I'm ready to listen to your suggestions."

"Come by the store tomorrow, and we'll talk about it." She turned to stare out her side window, effectively cutting Grant off from reading her face.

His plan to get her to forget that list and give him a chance had seemed so simple. But what if the walls they'd both built were just too big?

Caroline's gaze shifted from her office door, then back to her desk. Back to the door. Back to the desk. Talk about a manic Monday. Grant was supposed to stop by sometime today to resume their life coaching. Why hadn't she insisted on an appointment? Appointments, schedules, and lists made life run smooth. This was not smooth.

Why had she even agreed to be his life coach again? When he hadn't brought up the kiss and all that followed on the way home, she'd been so grateful that she said a quick yes to his question about life coaching. She really should have thought this through.

The growing collection of leaves by her monitor gave a solid testimony that she was already in too deep. The first ones had lost their rich color and curled at the edges. She lifted the one that he'd given her at the ranch and slid it between two pages of a thick book. Great. Now she was creating memorabilia.

Maybe it was time to make a new list—a to-do list, grocery list, anything-to-get-her-mind-off-Grant-and-keep-it-off list.

She pulled a mini light-blue legal pad from her drawer along with her purple pen. List. List. Her pen beat out a drumline rhythm on the desk.

Caroline squeezed her eyes shut. Focus. The only things coming into focus were Grant's deep blue-green eyes, wide shoulders, and the memory of the tattoo on his rib cage. The way he'd been staring at her in the bathroom. The distant look in his eyes when he'd talked about his dad at the ranch. She shook her head. She'd gotten over him before—she could get over him again.

The back door opened and slammed, and Caroline's pulse sped up. Would Grant use the back door? Her heart returned to its normal rhythm as Luke Johnson stepped into view, tool belt hung low on his hips and a smile across his beautiful face.

His dark eyes scanned the room. "Did you still need me to fix that shelf?"

"Right. It's over here." She cleared a few boxes and pointed to where the shelf had fallen off the wall over a month ago. Luke had been two years ahead of her in school and now served as the local handyman as he worked to complete an online degree. Nate would've probably fixed the shelf for free, but though Luke hadn't had an easy life, he never gave up. Hiring him for odd jobs now and then was the least she could do.

"Sorry it's taken me so long to get over here. Between classes and my house, it's been crazy." He stepped past her, pulled out a few tools, and got to work. That was Luke—a man of few words. He examined the shelf and then stood. "I need a wall anchor, but I think I have one in my truck."

Caroline picked up her legal pad and scanned it. Her list looked less like a list and more like a rough sketch of Grant's tattoo. This wasn't helping. She slammed it facedown on her desk and picked up Grant's file. Time to prepare for his meeting—the more prepared she was, the shorter she could make it.

She scanned her notes again. The words "security team" seemed to glow on the page. She'd found out that not only did they exist, but she'd also tracked down three companies for him to contact.

This would take him potentially all over the world. Her fingers itched to wad up the paper and pitch it in the trash, but he needed a job, and she needed him . . . away.

"So, spill." Leah leaned on the doorframe, eating salad out of a Tupperware container. "Where's your lunch?"

"I ordered delivery from Donny's. Who's watching out front?"

"I locked it." Leah dismissed her with a shake of the head, sending her red curls swinging. She dropped into the chair opposite Caroline. "I only have a few minutes left on my lunch break, and I want details."

Luke appeared again at Caroline's office door behind Leah.

"Did he kiss you?" Leah pulled her legs up under her.

Caroline gritted her teeth and stood. "Luke, did you find what you needed?"

Leah choked on her salad then covered her mouth as Luke walked around the desk.

He did his best to act like he hadn't overheard anything and offered Leah a million-dollar smile, showing off his dimple. "Hey, Leah." Then he knelt down and resumed his work.

Caroline gave her sister a pointed look. But Leah sat frozen, red-faced, watching Luke's every move. Poor Leah.

Yearning. See, this was what yearning looked like, and this was exactly why she wanted nothing to do with it. Why would Mason want this?

Luke was oblivious to her sister's ten-year crush. Not that she blamed him. He only had eyes for Hannah. Everyone could see that—but Hannah.

But this was exactly what she refused to turn into with Grant. Even if she tossed the list aside—which she wouldn't do—the guy didn't even want to get married. At all. She wouldn't fall for a guy with hopes that someday he'd come around and be ready to plan for the future.

The bell at the front door chimed.

"I thought you said you locked it."

"We practically live in Mayberry. What's going to happen?"

Grant rounded the doorframe.

Leah sighed and stood. "I'll get back out there, but we aren't done talking about this."

Caroline stood and focused on Grant as Leah disappeared out

the door. "Hi."

Yup, that was all she had. Her brain had turned to mush.

The smile she'd grown so fond of over the weekend tugged at the corner of his mouth as he slid out of his leather coat, laid it over a chair, and claimed his regular chair next to her desk.

"Did you figure out my future yet, Coach?" He eyed Luke on the floor.

"That's Luke. We can go somewhere else if you prefer."

Luke sat up and extended a hand. "Luke Johnson."

"Grant Quinn." Grant took Luke's hand as he seemed to size up Luke. "You should have told me you needed help, Caroline. I could've fixed that for you."

Was he jealous of Luke?

"No worries." Luke shrugged before leaning back under the shelf. "Almost done here."

Grant flexed his fingers and popped his neck.

He *was* jealous. Caroline pressed her lips together to keep from smiling. "Did you want to go somewhere else? Or come back later?"

"Now is good." Grant dismissed her question with a wave.

Caroline picked up the file and scanned it. "I need to be clear that I can't get you a job. I'm simply here to ask the right questions. Help you think about different options. Are you ready to tell me why the last job didn't work?"

The muscle in Grant's jaw worked as his gaze flicked to Luke and back. "No."

Of course not.

"Well, that makes this more difficult, but with your military experience, have you considered a private security team? They pay well, you're trained for it, and you did say you liked to travel. It might be a good fit." The words churned her. She was literally handing him a ticket out of her life. "Here's some information on three companies that are hiring."

Grant picked up the pages and leafed through them.

Caroline held her breath, willing her face to show no emotion.

"My buddy Jackson is working for this company—Eagle Eye Security. Maybe I'll give him a call." He leaned forward on his knees and studied his hands. "Do you want me to call him?"

Yes. No. She didn't know, but she did know that they needed to wrap up this conversation before she begged him to find a job in Heritage, even if it meant bagging groceries at JJ's Food Mart. "I want you to do what you want to do."

After a long pause, Grant locked eyes with her. "Go out with me this weekend."

"What?"

"You told me to do what I want. I want to go out with you this weekend. Not as my life coach or because we're trying to fool someone. Let's go out. You. Me."

The front bell chimed, and Caroline focused on her desk, shuffling the papers into orderly piles. Something dropped to the floor, but when she glanced down she didn't see it. She'd find it later.

The front bell chimed again as if shouting *Time's up*—seriously what was this, Grand Central Station?

Grant opened his mouth, but Nate appeared in the doorway. "Ready, buddy?"

Grant glanced from Caroline to Nate and back. "Almost."

Grant stared at her.

She stared back. "Grant, I think—"

"Olivia delivered this from Donny's." Leah rushed into the room and placed a white paper sack on Caroline's desk. Then rushed back toward the front.

Nate leaned out of her office and stared back down the hall. "Olivia? Is she still here?"

Leah's eyes strayed to Luke, who was now gathering his tools. "No, she said something about going somewhere with Hannah. I've got to get back out front."

Luke's head jerked around at Hannah's name.

Could there be more relational angst in one room? This is why appointments were a must. She analyzed her cousin, who still eyed the hall. So, Nate liked Olivia. When and how that had happened, she had no idea. But perhaps she could help *someone* today—and turn the conversation away from her and Grant. "You should ask her out."

"Who?" Nate, Grant, and Luke said in unison.

She looked straight at her cousin, lest Grant think she wanted him to ask someone else out. And really, she couldn't deal with Luke's and Hannah's drama today. "Olivia."

Nate's gaze skipped around the room. "I haven't been on a date in a long time. I'm not sure that's the way I want to start my job off here. A pastor dating can get . . . awkward."

Caroline shrugged. "So double. Find a couple of people and make it a group date."

"We'll do it." Grant leaned back in his chair and waited for her to object. "Right, Caroline?"

He was trying to corner her into a date, but it wasn't going to work.

She forced a smile. "Or Hannah could go with you. She owes me for canceling on you before."

A loud clang echoed through the room as the tool in Luke's hand hit the floor.

Everyone looked at Luke who stood up, red-faced. "Sorry. I think Hannah said she was busy that night."

Crossing her arms over her chest, Caroline lifted an eyebrow at him. "We didn't say what night."

"Right. My mistake. Shelf's fixed." He nodded once before he made a beeline for the door. "Oh, and I think you dropped this. It fell in my toolbox."

He held out a legal pad. The legal pad. Caroline's heart dropped. She reached for it, but Grant was between them. He took it from Luke and started to pass it to Caroline when he froze, his focus glued to the image. A smile slowly formed on his face.

"What do I owe you, Luke?" She needed to get out of here.

Luke just waved her off and disappeared down the hall. She started to step around Grant when he blocked her path, waving the notebook back and forth. She reached for it, but he pulled it back, keeping the list out of her reach. "So, do you want to go on a double date with them?"

What could she say? No. That's exactly what she could say. She turned to Nate, ready to do so, but his hopeful expression stopped her. "Sure."

Nate's face lit up as he hurried out the door. "Great. Maybe I'll go catch her now and see if she's free this Friday."

Caroline held out her hand to Grant. He didn't move. "I'm doing this as a favor to Nate. Not because I like you."

He waved the paper in the air. "This says you do."

"It doesn't say anything. It's just a drawing." Why did he look so smug?

"A drawing that seems quite familiar." Grant stood and took a step closer—so close that the warmth of his body set every inch of her on high alert. "I'm not sure why you're determined to fight this, Caroline."

The truth was she didn't know either, but her sanity seemed to depend on it. Falling for Grant would be falling into the great unknown with only her heart to lose.

He held the paper up between them, the clear replica of his tattoo drawn in purple ink. "But I'm glad to know you like it."

She closed her eyes as her heartbeat echoed in her ears.

He dropped the pad on her desk before turning toward the door. "One date, Caroline. That's all I'm asking for."

Maybe he was right. It was just one date. But that one date could cost her more than she was ready to give.

ten

This might be the worst first date in history—or was this technically their second date? Either way, Grant was ready to call it quits and start the ninety-minute drive back to Heritage. Holding the door for Caroline as they exited DeVos Performance Hall, he tried to make eye contact. No luck. She walked with her arms folded across her chest and her head down. The girl was a walking billboard for solitude. Too bad they were on a double date.

The rain from earlier had left the streets of Grand Rapids shining and the heavy, low clouds created a glow around the streetlights. He couldn't have planned a more romantic night. And with Caroline in that black dress and her hair pinned up, it almost reminded him of the engagement party. If only her goal for the evening wasn't to make it clear that she didn't want to be here, then it might have been perfect.

At least the night hadn't been a total bust. Nate and Olivia seemed to be having fun.

Olivia brushed her hand against Nate's arm. Leaning close, she whispered something in his ear. Nate turned back to her with a full smile. Now things were just getting awkward.

Olivia turned to them as Nate searched for something on his phone. "Do you want to walk across the Gillett Bridge? I hear the trees in Ah-Nab-Awen Park are perfect right now."

Sure. Why not drag out this torture a little longer? But Grant waited for Caroline to respond. She only gave him the briefest glance before her voice came out a bit too perky. "Great."

Olivia's smile dimmed slightly, but she turned toward the bridge. Enough was enough. Grant dropped his hand onto Caroline's shoulder. Her muscles stiffened under his touch. "Why don't you two go ahead. We'll catch up."

Nate nodded, claimed Olivia's hand, and started away. "Text if you're ready to go but haven't found us."

Caroline shot Grant a glare, but he ignored it and turned her the opposite way down the sidewalk. "I get you don't want to be on a date with me, but Nate and Olivia do deserve a chance to have fun."

Caroline crossed her arms tight across her chest. "Did you get the email I sent for the website content?"

"Yes. But we aren't talking business tonight." He paused and pointed down a street. "This will lead to the bridge as well."

She looked like she was about to argue, but Grant just held up his hands and stepped back. "Don't worry. Your message has come across loud and clear. I don't know why you're suddenly afraid of me. But fear not, I won't even try to hold your hand. They're staying in the pockets."

Her shoulders slumped as they walked the rest of the way to the bridge in silence.

Halfway across the bridge, Caroline paused and leaned on the rail, staring over the water. "I'm sorry, Grant. I . . . I don't know what's wrong with me. I just . . ."

Grant stopped next to her. "Have a plan and I'm not a part of it."

"Something like that."

Did she really think she'd find happiness following these lists?

Grant leaned his elbows next to her. "I could be wrong, but we had fun last weekend. All pretending to date aside, I had a good time hanging out with you."

"I'm not good at the whole boy-girl thing. Blame my parents' dysfunctional marriage, blame my obsession as a child with fairy tales, blame the guy who broke my heart when I was young—"

"I'm pretty sure that was me."

She poked him in the shoulder as a smile tugged at the corner of her lips. "Yeah, blame yourself."

She pushed away from the edge and continued walking across the bridge. "Even Mason once said I was as affectionate as a cold fish. Nice, right?"

Was she kidding? A memory of the one real kiss they shared filled his mind. Grant stepped in her path and waited until she looked up. "After last weekend—which I'm still in debt to you for, by the way—trust me, Caroline, when I say you're not a cold fish."

Her eyes widened as they darted to his lips and then back to his eyes. Her cheeks reddened slightly. "That . . . that was pretend."

He offered a half shrug. "Maybe. What happened to the girl from the notes who shared everything she felt?"

"She was too honest." The color in her cheeks deepened to a sweet cherry color.

"Why were you living with Nate that summer?"

She stepped around him and continued across the bridge. "My father traveled for business, and it was hard on my parents' marriage. My mother made a last-ditch effort that summer to travel with him to see if they could save the marriage. They couldn't."

"So, where did you end up after that summer?"

"My mom moved us in with my grandparents in Heritage that fall. She got sick right away. Her doctors weren't completely sure what it was. A virus from her travels they said. She passed away before Christmas."

Grant's heart pinched at the image of thirteen-year-old Caroline dealing with the death of her mother. "I'm sorry."

"My grandparents were awesome. They made their house ours, and I felt as if I had a real home for the first time. Leah and I started helping my grandparents run the business in high school and then took it over when my grandfather passed away during our third year of college. My grandma died less than a year later. I don't think she knew what to do without him."

"You ran the shop and went to college at the same time?"

"It was a lot to balance—school and the shop—but we managed."

Dots began to scatter across the cement. Grant eyed the darkening sky. Great—rain. He sent a quick text to Nate then turned them back the way they had come. "What about your dad?"

"His check came very faithfully until Leah's and my eighteenth birthday."

His steps paused. "He didn't make an effort to see you? Even after your mom died?"

"No." She kept walking. "Getting mom pregnant with David when she was eighteen hadn't really been part of his plan. Then a few years later they got a little tipsy one night, and a set of twin girls showed up nine months later—definitely not a part of his plan. My mom, on the other hand, wasn't into planning anything and seemed to believe that somehow it'd all work out. It didn't."

"Which is why you're obsessed with planning."

"You have to see that a lack of planning leads to mistakes, heartache, and a life people don't want."

"Maybe, but a lack of planning also led to your existence on the planet, and that's one poor planning that I'm thankful for." Grant stopped in front of Caroline until she met his gaze once more. "I'm not saying that planning is bad. It's just, 'No plan survives contact with the enemy.'"

"What?"

"It's a famous quote by Helmuth von Moltke, a German general in the nineteenth century. I'm guessing it isn't an exact quote, since I suppose he spoke German. But you get the idea. In the military, we had to have a plan going into every situation. But we also knew that plan would change the minute our boots hit the ground. The enemy was unpredictable, and how my team would adjust to the enemy's actions wasn't always predictable. If we held to the plan too tightly, then failure was the usual outcome."

"So, you choose not to plan in your life, to ensure that you never fail."

Is that what he was doing?

"What happened with that job interview, Grant?"

Grant closed his eyes a moment and dug his hands deeper into his pockets. "The situation contained elements that created a less than ideal work environment."

"What?"

Yeah—he wasn't quite sure what he'd said either. He drew a breath and opened his mouth to try again, when the skies opened up with a roar as rain pelted down. Grant grabbed her hand and pulled her the rest of the way across the bridge and under an awning of one of the businesses.

Caroline pushed the wet hair from her face. "I'm a mess."

"You look like you did that night at Nate's." Grant stepped closer and lifted a wet curl plastered on her face and tucked it behind her ear, letting his fingers linger on her jaw.

She stilled at his touch, her eyes fixed on him, conveying a very different message than she had earlier.

Maybe he should kiss her senseless and see if she still wanted to deny anything was going on.

Okay, that would be a jerk move after he'd told her she could trust him not to hit on her, but what would she do if he kissed her right now? Not because they were putting on a show, but because she liked him and he liked her. And right now that was all that mattered.

He ran his thumb along her jaw, catching a rogue drip of water. Her breath caught as her gaze darted from his eyes to his mouth and back to his eyes.

She had no idea how difficult she was making this. She made him forget any dream he once had about the military, and thank the good Lord above that he'd failed his eye exam so he could have this minute. Here.

He leaned a fraction closer—

"Caroline?" A deep voice filled their hideaway.

Caroline blinked at her name. Her eyes widened and her face paled as she focused on their new guest.

Grant followed her gaze to a midsize man with a man bun and hipster clothes. The expression that crossed the guy's face as he studied Caroline made Grant want to pull her closer—and maybe punch the guy.

Grant glanced at Caroline.

She stared at the man with an unreadable expression. "Hello, Mason."

Mason? Perfect-guy-that-got-a-check-in-every-category Mason? The jerk-who-broke-her-heart-after-four-years Mason?

"Wow. I can't believe I ran into you here of all places. How are you? You look good."

As Mason's gaze trailed over Caroline, Grant clenched his hand to keep from pushing the guy back into the rain.

Two girls rushed out of the rain under an umbrella behind him.

"Seriously, Mason. How fast do you think we can go in heels?" A petite blonde with a heavy amount of makeup and a low-cut blouse narrowed her eyes at Mason.

Mason shrugged. "I gave you the umbrella."

"That's my brother—probably worried about his hair," the brunette in the back murmured as she shook the rain off her clothes.

The blonde stared Caroline down with a cat-fight challenge in her eyes as she slid her arm through Mason's. "Caroline. Fancy meeting you here."

Her glare seemed to accuse Caroline of arranging this little rendezvous. *Jealous much?*

The other girl stared at Grant. He offered her an awkward nod and prayed the rain would let up—soon.

Caroline blinked, stepped closer to Grant, and entwined their fingers. "I'm great. This is Grant. Grant, this is Mason and Melissa, and Mason's sister, Becca." She motioned to the one still staring at him.

He rubbed his fingers against the softness of Caroline's hand. He'd been longing to reach for it all night, but she'd pushed him away—until Mason showed up. He couldn't begrudge the action. After all, they'd just spent a weekend at his mother's house putting on the same show. And the look in Melissa's eyes seemed a little too smug.

He owed Caroline, and he wasn't going to let her down now. Grant put his arm around her shoulders, tugging her close. "It's nice to meet you."

If Caroline's reaction to seeing Mason with another girl was any indication, she was not over Mason. And if she was still in love with the guy, he needed to face the fact she wasn't into him—at least not enough.

She wasn't a violent person but hanging around Grant seemed to be changing that. First Melanie and now Becca. The girl couldn't stop looking at him. Caroline leaned further into Grant and glared again at Becca.

The girl didn't pay Caroline any attention. All she did was focus on Grant and fill the air with never-ending questions. Caroline should be thankful there was something to break up the awkward silence as they all stood together trapped by the rain, but how much could she take of *What do you do, Grant? Wow, you were in the military? You must be strong. I'd love to hear more about it.*

As if Caroline's presence was a mere inconvenience. Maybe it was. With Becca's traffic-stopping figure and a face that could grace the cover of a magazine, the girl could have any guy she wanted, and she knew it.

Caroline glanced at Mason again. The list had said he was perfect, but standing here seeing Mason next to Grant, she couldn't remember why she'd believed it was true.

It wasn't just physical—that landed Grant in clear first place—but with Grant, there was something about him that stood out.

The way his body had stiffened to high alert the instant Mason had said her name, as if ready to take him out if she'd given him the right signal. The way his arm had wrapped around her shoulders when Mason stared at her. The way his thumb offered a soothing touch on her shoulder blade every time Melissa shot her a glare.

Grant was her protector—her warrior—and she never felt safer than when she was with him. Not just physically safe—which was obvious—but like he'd do anything to help her fight the demons of her past, navigate her problems of today, and help her find a new smile for tomorrow.

Mason had always been about . . . Mason.

How had she ever thought she loved him?

But Grant? She loved him. Her body and mind flooded with a hurricane of emotions as the truth settled in. She loved Grant.

She honestly—without a doubt—loved him.

"How's the WIFI going, Caroline?" Mason's voice cut off

Becca's next question.

Right. Probably this wasn't the best time to confess her love.

She focused back on Mason. "Fine."

What was there to say? The question was as odd as his texts had been. Wait. Did Melissa even know that Mason had texted her a few days ago?

Maybe they weren't together as much as Melissa thought. Or maybe it was a new thing.

She turned her attention to Melissa. "So, how long have you two been together?"

Mason's eyes widened. "It's recent."

"Four months." Melissa's words overlapped his.

Always count on the girl for detailed information.

Wait.

Four months?

Mason had dumped her not even two months ago. Four months ago, Mason had still been in China. The truth hit her square in the chest. Mason had mentioned a team visiting from the States. He may have even mentioned Melissa's name.

Caroline pinned Mason with her gaze. Guilt dripped from Mason's expression before he looked down at his feet. The no-good cheater.

Grant's bicep tightened as if he'd done the math as well. Grant was a better man in every way and a better man for her.

If a jerk like Mason was an A on her carefully constructed list, then maybe her whole approach to life was flawed.

Caroline looked up at Grant. "I think the rain is stopping. We should go."

And even if it were still pouring, she'd rather be out there with Grant than here under this awning with Mason.

He nodded and offered his goodbyes.

"I'd love to hear more about your time in the military. I'm thinking about writing a book, and I'd love your insight." Becca wrote something on a paper and slipped it into his hand. "Call me."

Caroline tightened her grip on Grant's hand and resisted the urge to rip the paper away and toss it in the trash.

Grant smiled politely and shoved it into his pocket. *His pocket.*

Caroline drew a deep breath. Words were beyond her. He'd put Becca's number in his pocket. They passed a trash can on their left. He kept walking.

Grant pulled his hand away from Caroline. "I'm sorry about that."

He was sorry? About taking a girl's number on their date?

"It'll get easier. Trust me."

Easier? Did a lot of girls hand him numbers on dates? Why wasn't he throwing that away?

"Being cheated on stinks, but he's the idiot."

Wait, what? Right. Mason had as much as admitted that he'd been cheating on her for the last couple months of their relationship. The snake.

A fact that should bother her more than it did.

Three months ago she'd gone ring shopping with the guy, and today she could care less if he was dating Melissa or every girl at his church.

What was wrong with her?

Maybe if she'd heard that he'd cheated before she'd come to her great revelation, it would've stung more. But now? Now all she could think about was keeping Grant away from Becca. And how to get that number out of his pocket. He might notice if she reached in his pocket to grab it.

She had to tell him how she felt. Get it out in the open. Find out if he really wanted to call Becca.

Caroline paused and turned toward him. She shifted from one foot to the other, aware of how with every nerve, every cell, every thought she wanted to throw her arms around his neck and kiss him like she had at the party.

Maybe she should.

"I get it." Grant took a half step back.

"What?"

"Jealousy catches us off guard sometimes. Did you have any idea that he was cheating?"

Wait. Were they back to Mason again? "I'm not upset about that."

She should be. What a jerk. But really—Mason next to Grant?

No contest.

"It's okay to admit you were a bit jealous." Grant lifted an eyebrow in her direction. "That's why you dropped into pretend mode like at the engagement party, right?"

"Pretend mode?" She hadn't even thought about it. It hadn't felt like pretending. Had it seemed like pretending to him?

"Don't worry about it. It's cool. We're cool." Grant tucked that wayward piece of hair behind her ear again before shoving his hand in his pocket.

Man, she wished he lingered like last time.

She'd been trying to push him away for a week, and it seemed he'd finally listened only now that she knew she wanted him.

She stepped in front of him as he turned toward the car. "I'm serious. I don't have feelings for Mason."

A look of doubt passed over his face. He shrugged and continued walking. "Let's go find Olivia and Nate."

She planted her hands on her hips and blocked his path again. How could she explain if he wouldn't listen?

Maybe kissing him was the only option. She'd been spontaneous once. She could do it again. Right? She stepped closer. This time, she'd finish that kiss.

His turquoise eyes filled with his own questions. She could do this. Another step closer. Deep breath. Her mouth went dry as her pulse pounded in her ears. She licked her drying lips. Being spontaneous was easier when she didn't take the time to think about it.

Caroline reached up and traced the scar over his eye with one finger. Grant's eyes shut with her movement and his body leaned toward her.

"Grant! Caroline!" Nate shouted from down the walk.

Both took a step back as the couple approached.

Nate pulled his keys from his pocket. "The rain is picking up again. Ready to go?"

Was it raining again? Sure enough, a steady light rain fell, and by the way her curls dripped water, it hadn't just started.

"We'd better run for it before it starts pouring again." Olivia tugged Nate's arm.

Too late. The sky opened up as the four ran for the car. Caroline climbed in the back next to Grant, both soaking wet. She pulled her phone from her coat pocket to make sure it had stayed dry, then set it on her lap.

He stared at her, then placed his hand on the seat between them but looked out the front. What she wouldn't give to have just a few more minutes alone with him to make sure he understood.

She rested her hand next to his, close but not touching. The light brush of his pinky finger on hers set every nerve singing.

Her phone buzzed from her lap, and it took Caroline a second to register what it was. Really? She glanced at her phone and froze.

MASON

I need to see you.

Caroline scooped it up before Grant could see. She started to shut it off when another text came in.

MASON

I found your grandma's necklace.

Grant leaned forward to say something to Nate.

She held the phone close and typed out a quick text.

CAROLINE

When?

MASON

I can bring it over tonight?

Was the guy delusional? No way!

CAROLINE

No.

Donny's tomorrow at noon.

MASON

Can't wait.

See you then.

She dropped her phone into her purse and turned back to Grant. He'd leaned back into the seat, the same position he'd been in before, but with his arms crossed. Had he seen the text? She needed to explain but not here. They could try to whisper, but it would still be awkward in front of Nate and Olivia. She'd call him tonight after they were all home.

"Olivia and I talked about watching a movie when we get back. Can you believe she has never seen *Better Off Dead*?" Nate glanced at them in the rearview mirror.

"Not everyone is as obsessed with John Cusack as you are, Nate."

"They should be. The guy's movies are classic. You two want to join us?"

"Sorry," Grant spoke up before Caroline could even consider it. He closed his eyes, sank down further into his seat, and tipped his head back. "Running at quarter to five comes early. I'm already barely staying awake."

Caroline swallowed the lump that rose in her throat. So much for talking later tonight or even sharing a few whispers on the way home. He'd effectively cut off all earlier connection.

Whatever had caused the shift, she had to fix it. And soon. But how could she do that if she didn't know what had gone wrong?

eleven

No matter how he played it in his head, Grant still came out on the losing end. He dug his shoes into the gravel and pushed himself faster as if he could outrun the memory of last night, but his legs burned in protest. He'd taken the long route today, and after pushing himself hard the past nine miles, he wasn't sure he had the final one in him.

He slowed his pace, tipped his head back, and drew a quick gulp from his water bottle. Just enough to keep him from cramping, then he picked up speed again.

If Nate and Olivia hadn't interrupted his moment with Caroline, last night might have ended very differently—who was he kidding, it *would* have ended very differently. But the interruption had been for the best. No matter how much he liked kissing her, he preferred it not being a knee-jerk reaction to finding out Mason had cheated on her.

She'd claimed she hadn't been jealous, and he'd wanted to believe her. He almost had when she'd licked the edge of her lips and ran her finger down his scar.

But he couldn't dismiss the text. He had tried not to look, and he hadn't seen much. Just Mason's name and her words *Donny's tomorrow at noon* followed by the reply of *Can't wait. See you then.*

So that was that.

Grant stopped in front of Nate's house and checked his pulse. He downed the rest of his water, stretched his hamstrings, and headed inside for more water.

Now what? Stay in Heritage? Not likely. She had given him the number for the security team—code for you can leave my life now, please.

He'd always assumed that he'd jump at the chance to do field work again—be on a team again—but nothing in him wanted to dial that number. Caroline had changed him. Made him want more. A home. A family.

But Caroline didn't want him. Or at least not as her first choice, and he didn't like playing runner-up.

Grant downed a full glass of water and then filled it again before heading toward his room.

He snatched up his phone and dialed the number before he changed his mind. Three rings later a familiar voice answered. "Eagle Eye Security. This is Cooper."

Grant dropped onto the edge of his bed. "Coop? Is that really you?"

"Who's this?"

"Grant Quinn."

"Quinn. What are you up to? Please tell me you're looking for a job. We need you, buddy."

"Maybe."

"You're killing me. When is the soonest you can get here?"

Grant rubbed his fingers over his scar. "You're ready to give me a job, just like that?"

"Eh, there's an interview process and paperwork, but both Jackson and Conway are here, too, and with the three of us vouching for you, you're in."

Grant stood and leaned his elbows against the window. The rain last night had brought down a layer of leaves that now blanketed the yard. "Tell me about the job."

"The position we're looking for now is someone to head up the European team. You'd be perfect."

Europe? Talk about a jaunt from Heritage.

"You don't have anything holding you there, do you?"

Grant turned his back to the window and rubbed his forehead. "No."

"I'll tell you what. Why don't I fly you out, and we can talk. No harm in that. Can I get you on a flight tonight?"

"Tonight?"

"They're already interviewing guys from all over. We don't have time to sit on this."

When Grant didn't answer, Cooper spoke again. "What's your closest city?"

"Grand Rapids, Michigan."

"Great." The click of computer keys carried through the phone. "There's a flight at five-thirty. What's your full name, birth date, and email?"

Grant rattled off his information, then ended the call. Cooper was right—it didn't hurt to check it out. Especially on their dime.

He pulled his duffel bag from the closet and dropped it on the bed.

Nate poked his head into the room, a basketball under his arm. "Up for a game?"

"Can't. Any chance you can give me a ride to the airport?"

"Now?" Nate glanced at his watch. "Where're you going?"

"I'm checking out a job in Europe."

The ball dropped from Nate's hands. "You're flying to Europe?"

Grant pulled open his top drawer and grabbed out a stack of T-shirts. "No. The main base is in Florida." He picked up the ball and tossed it back to Nate. "But the position they're looking to fill is in Europe."

Nate caught the ball and spun it on his finger. "Wow. That's cool."

"Yup."

"You must be excited."

"Yup."

Nate shoved the ball back under his arm. "You don't sound excited."

Grant sorted through his pants and added a few to the growing pile on the bed.

Nate spun the ball a few times, but he didn't leave. "I thought when we talked the other night you weren't sure you wanted to be that far away."

"Things change."

"Things with Caroline?"

Grant didn't answer. He yanked open the drawer that held his shorts. Maybe Nate would get the idea he didn't want to talk.

"You two looked pretty cozy when we found you last night."

"That was before she decided to meet Mason today."

"What?" The ball hit the floor as Nate dropped onto the bed, disrupting several of the piles. "Are they back together?"

"Seems that way."

"Wait. Did she say they were?"

Grant paused his search through his socks but didn't answer.

Nate stood and shoved the ball back under his arm and shook his head. "You know you're like a brother, which is why I've gotta say this. You're a mess. Ever since you showed up on my doorstep, your emotions are like shifting sand. You're running away from something you won't talk about, and you refuse to run toward anything. You need an anchor, man."

"Like God?" Grant couldn't keep the sarcasm from his voice as he picked up a shirt and refolded it.

"You may think that your life was supposed to turn out differently—that somehow God failed you, but He didn't. Junk happens. Not just to you. You can either choose to see how God wants to use that pain in your life or be angry." Nate snapped his fingers and pointed at him. "Jacob."

"What?" Grant added the shirt to his duffel and reached for another.

"Jacob. Jacob's life wasn't going according to plan. First, he has to run for his life so his brother doesn't kill him. Then he works for seven years to marry the wrong girl. Then his father-in-law starts getting jealous of his success. But guess what? God had never left him. In fact, God used all that to build the twelve tribes. Grant, God has a plan He wants to work out in your life, and you can let Him, or you can fight Him."

"I'm not fighting Him. I'm just doing my own thing." He inspected another shirt, shook it out, and folded it again.

"And how's that working out for you?"

"Fine."

"I want more out of my life than *fine*. I thought you did too."

Why was everyone against the word *fine*? Grant smoothed the shirt again. It still bunched. "Yeah, well, I went for more and failed."

"Try again."

Grant shook out the shirt once more with more force. "Are you saying that you think I should take this job, or are you saying I should go after Caroline?"

"I'm saying don't leave because you're running away from something. Figure out what you want and run toward it." He checked his watch. "I'm off to shoot hoops. What time is your flight?"

"I need to leave here between twelve and one."

Nate nodded and disappeared out the door.

Grant wadded the shirt and threw it on the bed.

His phone buzzed from the dresser as a text from an unknown number rolled in.

UNKNOWN

This is Seth.

Seth? Why did that name sound familiar. Probably wrong number or spam.

Nice to meet you, Seth. I'll now delete you. Grant's finger hovered over the delete key when another text came in.

UNKNOWN

You wrote your number in my drawing book.

Right. Grant tapped at the screen.

GRANT

The guy who could draw dragons.

What's up?

SETH

You really know a way to quit?

Was this God's way of telling him he should stay?

GRANT

Want to talk?

SETH

Where?

GRANT

Donny's. Noon.

That still gave him time to make his flight. And maybe he'd drop by the WIFI to talk to Caroline and decide if he wanted to make that flight or not.

His phone vibrated again, and he looked at the display.

SETH

Sure

Maybe

The answer wasn't as solid as he wanted, but he'd be waiting. After all, Grant understood the *maybes* of life. Maybe he'd stop by Caroline's. Maybe he'd take the flight. Maybe he'd someday stop fighting God. Today he'd deal with Seth's *maybe.*

How could a day go so wrong? Caroline shoved her phone into her purse and slid into a booth at Donny's. Grant still wasn't answering his phone, and now she had to talk with Mason. Donny's was a flurry of lunchtime rush, which was why she'd wanted to meet here.

There was no way she'd wanted him to come to her house last night, nor to meet him at some secluded place today. She didn't really want to see him at all, but she needed her necklace, and if he needed closure—or whatever—she'd give it to him. But it would be here, on her territory.

After this meeting, this chapter of her life could be finally closed. Hopefully, he didn't ask about his CD that was still on the floor of her car.

The door jingled as Mason entered the diner with a swagger. He closed the distance from the door to her booth in four strides and a too confident grin. *Ugh.* She turned away. His lips landed on her cheek, and she jerked back and glared at him, but he didn't seem to notice.

Mason slid in across from her. "Same ole Donny's."

She turned and grabbed the nearest waitress. "Excuse me. We're ready to order when you have a second." Then she turned back to Mason and held out her hand. "My necklace."

He reached out and took her hand in his. "First, let's talk."

She pulled her hand back and glared at him again, but he continued. "I'm sorry for how I ended things. I wasn't sure what I wanted, or if I was ready for the future you had all laid out for us. You have to admit, it was a bit intense. But lately, I've really missed you, and after seeing you last night with Gary—"

"Grant."

"I made a huge mistake in letting you go. I want you. I want us. We're great together."

"Can I please have my necklace?"

Some of the confidence faded from his eyes. "You can't be serious about Gabe."

"Grant.

"He isn't right for you, and you know it." One eyebrow lifted as he crossed his arms. "Military? The guy has 'wanderer' written all over him. That's the last thing you want."

Her gut churned at his words. After all, a week ago she would've agreed. Three weeks ago she might've jumped at the chance to get back together with Mason, but now? Now the only thing she was sure of was Grant. "Maybe you don't know me as well as you think."

"That isn't true, and you know it." He released a frustrated sigh and set a white heart-shaped box on the table between them.

The box looked more like a ring box than one that held a necklace. This was bad. Very bad.

His gaze and voice softened. "I do know you. And I know we're perfect for each other."

It wasn't Mason's fault that he thought he knew her now. Mason did know a piece of her, but she'd been very careful about what she'd allowed him to see. She'd never opened her heart to him like she had to Grant in those letters way back when. She hadn't really opened herself to anyone that much since.

"We're perfect for each other. Deep down, you know it too, Caroline." He flipped the box open and slid it across the table. "Marry me?"

She wanted to believe he wasn't serious, but the three-thousand-dollar princess-cut solitaire in front of her told another story. She looked up to speak, but words wouldn't come. She looked back at the ring. Back to Mason.

"It's the one we picked out together, remember? I had it sized and everything. Try it on." Mason reached for the ring and lifted it out toward her.

That snapped her out of it. "No."

"No?" Mason's brow furrowed as if he didn't understand the easiest translated word in all languages.

"No." Caroline spoke slow and clear to help him out.

He stared at her a moment before confidence returned to his eyes. "You don't mean that. I've seen your lists. I'm exactly what you're looking for. I've seen your plan."

"'No plan survives contact with the enemy.'" Grant's words came back to her and tumbled out her mouth.

He replaced the ring into the box. "Did you just call me the enemy?"

"No, it's a saying. It's just . . . my list is stupid."

His nostrils flared as he steepled his fingers in front of his face. "Will you pray about it at least?"

This she didn't need to pray about because, even if Grant didn't exist, Mason was not what she wanted.

"Mason, I think you were right a month ago when you called it quits. I didn't—don't—yearn for you, and you admitted that you don't feel that way about me either."

"You're the one who always said emotions were overrated."

"I don't feel that way anymore."

"You're saying that after only one date, you yearn for Grant?" His hand tightened into a fist, but at least he'd gotten the name right. "I don't believe you."

"You don't have to." Caroline held up her hand. "There's nothing you can say that will make me change my mind." She pushed the box across the table.

Mason didn't pick it up, but instead reached in his pocket and pulled out her necklace. "Here. But I want you to think about it, Caroline. We're good together."

She took the necklace as their food arrived.

Mason asked the waitress for his to go and dropped enough cash to cover his food on the table. "You think you've changed. But you're a girl who's glued to her lists and plans. I know you. And when Grant stops being the shiny new penny and leaves you to seek another adventure, you'll see I'm right."

He marched toward the door, nearly plowing over the busboy as he went.

She *had* changed, whether Mason wanted to see it or not. And Grant wasn't a shiny new penny. But the idea of Grant leaving her for his next adventure lodged in her chest.

She rubbed at her temple to dislodge a building headache.

Hannah, eyes wide, slid into Mason's vacated spot. "Did Mason propose to you?"

Olivia dropped into the booth next to Hannah, her arms full of menus.

"Where did you two come from?" Caroline stared at one friend then the other.

Olivia lifted the menus. "I'm just starting my shift."

Hannah shrugged and pointed at the counter where a coffee mug sat abandoned. "I was . . . drinking coffee."

"You were spying on me?"

"No." Hannah pointed at her. "I was providing back up. Which gets back to the question. Did Mason propose to you?"

Caroline nodded at her friends as she pushed the food aside.

"It was awful. Even after I said no, he sat there staring at me, telling me how I'd eventually change my mind."

"Wait." Hannah looked at Olivia, then resumed staring at Caroline. "You said no?"

"Of course I said no. I still can't believe I thought I wanted to marry him."

"Was it a solid no?" Olivia's forehead wrinkled. "Or a let-me-think-about-it no?"

"Solid no." Caroline covered her face with her hands. "How did I get things so wrong? I mean, on paper he was perfect."

"That's why you don't date paper dolls." Olivia crossed her arms. "God's way doesn't always make sense on paper, but it's often the best journey."

Caroline glanced at Hannah, who seemed just as confused. "What's that from, a greeting card?"

"Facebook meme—but it fits." Olivia shook her head and again shared a look with Hannah.

When Hannah shrugged, Caroline slammed her hand on the table. "What's with you two?"

They exchanged one more look before Hannah spoke up. "You're confident that Mason knew it was a solid no, right?"

"Yes. Why?"

They pointed to the middle of the table where the princess-cut solitaire still sat. Caroline dropped her head in her hands and massaged at both temples now as a headache arrived full force. So much for this chapter of her life finally being closed.

twelve

He was batting a thousand today, wasn't he? Grant had frozen in the door of Donny's as Mason held out a diamond ring to Caroline. He gave the room a once-over, and not seeing Seth, turned and headed back outside.

Why hadn't he remembered Caroline was meeting Mason here?

His blood pulsed through his ears, and he struggled to swallow. Mason and Caroline engaged.

Movement across the street caught his eye. Seth sat on the step of an old abandoned house, hood pulled low, backpack slung over his left shoulder, rolling something between his fingers.

No. Grant had one more thing to do before he left.

"Hey, Seth." Grant lifted his voice to cover the distance.

Seth's head snapped up. A flicker of surprise crossed his face before he masked it behind a scowl.

Grant crossed the street and dropped down onto the step next to Seth. "What do you say to getting something to eat? It's my treat."

Seth sat up a little straighter at that but then eyed a group of teens dressed a lot like him approaching the diner, laughing a little louder than necessary. Seth sunk lower and turned his face away from the kids. "Maybe this was a mistake."

"Maybe. Or maybe not."

"I think I want to quit," Seth finally said as he stared at the weed in his hand.

Grant lifted one eyebrow. "You think you do?"

Seth shrugged without looking up.

Grant leaned forward, propping his elbows on his knees. "To be honest, when it comes to quitting addiction, you need a strong resolve, or it'll be too easy to return to it when the going gets tough. And trust me when I say it will get tough."

Seth shifted.

"So what happened that made you want to quit?" Grant couldn't lose the opening he had, but he could see the doors closing on him.

Seth pushed to a stand. "I gotta go."

"Text me anytime."

"Yeah . . . sure . . ." Seth mumbled the words as he turned away from the road and ducked between the broken-down houses.

That couldn't have gone worse.

The door to the diner opened and Caroline exited alone. She turned toward the WIFI with her head down as she tapped at the screen of her phone. His phone started buzzing next to him.

Grant declined the call. They needed to talk, but not by phone.

His phone rang again. Nate.

"Hey, Nate. Can you still give me a ride?"

"Still going?"

"Yup."

"Okay. Meet me at the house in thirty minutes."

Grant glanced at the time. "Perfect. I've one stop to make, and then I'll be there."

Grant stood and made his way to the WIFI. When he pushed through the door, Leah greeted him. "Hey, stranger. Caroline's in her office."

Grant nodded and walked toward the back, knocked twice on her door, and stepped in. She wasn't in there. Maybe she was in the storage room. Should he go look for her or sit and wait?

He scanned the room as if it held the answer. Her purse was here. His gaze moved on but snapped back. A familiar white box sat to the right of her purse.

He'd only seen it for a split second, but he'd recognize the cheesy heart shape anywhere. He'd actually held on to a shred of hope that she'd said no. Well, this was his answer. After all, she wouldn't have taken the ring unless she was at least thinking about it. Either way, it was enough to tell Grant what he needed to know.

"You're here." Caroline paused in front of him and then hesitated before biting at the corner of her lip. "We need to talk."

"Yeah, we do. I called Eagle Eye Security. I'm flying down for an interview. It's pretty much a done deal, so I wanted to say thank you for all your help. I'm not sure when I'll be up this way again."

All color drained from Caroline's face just before it flushed. She stepped around him and sat, straightening papers at her desk. "I'm glad I could help. Let me know how it goes."

When she looked up, a professional expression had erased any emotion. If there had been any. "Best of luck to you."

Right. Guess he was being dismissed.

"You too. You'll make a fine life coach."

She smiled a little too big to be real and picked up a pen and tapped it against the legal pad.

Was she even going to tell him about the engagement? "Did you want to talk to me about something?"

Her face went blank before she recovered. "Another job possibility, but it doesn't sound like you need it."

"A job? Okay then." If that was how she wanted to play it—whatever. His gaze paused on the ring box as he turned toward the door. "I guess I'll see you around."

The tapping of her pen stopped. "Wait."

He kept walking. He wouldn't let a girl make a fool of him again.

An hour ago she'd been ready to hand him her heart—how could she have been so foolish? Caroline dropped her pen and stood with such force that her chair rocked back before righting itself with a thud. "Just wait."

Grant paused in the door but didn't turn around.

"You saw the ring. Didn't you?" She tried to control the waver in her voice but failed.

He turned around and offered the slightest nod as he worked his jaw.

She leaned on her desk to keep from shaking. He'd seen the ring and thought the worst of her without even asking for an explanation. Hadn't she told him yesterday that she didn't like Mason? But instead of even giving her a chance to explain, he was taking the first escape he found. "And now you're going to Florida?"

He shifted his weight to the other foot and pulled keys from his pocket. "It's a position in Europe actually."

She dropped back in her chair. She pressed her hand to her chest as she stared at her desk through unshed tears. She took a few steadying breaths as the unspoken words filled the room and squeezed the air out of her lungs.

Grant took a half step toward her. "Are you *really* marrying him? Do you love . . . him?"

How could he think that? Caroline opened her mouth, but nothing came out. Was she really willing to trust her heart to a guy who ran at the first hint of trouble? "Does it matter? You're headed to Europe."

Grant stared at her, and his jaw twitched.

She blinked hard. She wouldn't cry. She definitely wouldn't beg him to stay. She'd seen her mother do both, too many times. "Have a safe trip."

"So that's it?"

"From the beginning, I told you it wouldn't work." Her voice wavered but only a touch. He had to leave soon, or she wouldn't be able to hold back the tears any longer.

"I never really had a chance with you, did I?" Grant shook his head, raking both hands through his hair. "I'm not your dad, Caroline. But I'm also not perfect either, and I can't have a life with you looking over my shoulder making a checklist of all my failures."

"And I can't live a life with someone who runs away whenever life hits a bump. Can't have the assignment you want? Quit the Army. Don't like the way things are going at home? Run to Heritage. Job interview not go the way you want it? Leave—"

"I didn't leave the interview because it wasn't going my way."

"How would I know? You still haven't told me why. For a person who values honesty so much—you're *really* bad at it." Her voice echoed off the walls of the small office.

"Honesty? You want to talk to me about honesty? How about your little performance last night and then this." He pointed at the ring box.

"Here's a little honesty for you. I think it's time for you to run away to your next adventure."

"I think you're right." He marched toward the front door, tearing her heart out with every step. The bell announced his final departure from her life. She shut the office door and turned the lock just before she sank to the floor. She wrapped her arms around her knees, buried her face, and let the tears flow.

There was a soft tapping on glass followed by the rattling of the doorknob. "Caroline? Caroline, let me in."

She'd let Leah in later. Right now she needed to just sob and forget why she ever thought yearning for someone was a good idea.

After twenty minutes, all she had to show was a pile of Kleenexes and a pair of red, swollen eyes. But no matter how much she cried, the pain didn't lessen. Every inch of her throbbed and ached as if she were fighting the flu.

Rule number one—No wallowing.

Wait, maybe that was Rule number three.

Whatever.

Caroline scanned over her to-do list. Stocking shelves was about all she was good for. She went to the storage room and found the box she needed.

"You're really going to let him leave?" Leah stepped in front of Caroline as she made her way toward the postcard carousel.

Caroline hiked the box higher on her hip and glared at her sister. "Stay out of it."

Caroline tried to move around her, but Leah blocked her path again, hands on her hips like her own personal barricade. "Why didn't you tell him that you said *no* to Mason? Or that you love him? Or anything?"

Caroline dropped the box. "Eavesdrop much?"

"I'm not sure it's eavesdropping when your voices carry down the hall. You need to go after him."

"No, I don't."

"Why? Grant's amazing. He's—"

"Just like Dad." The words scraped against her throat. The signs were all there. She picked up the box and waited for Leah to step aside.

Leah's brow wrinkled. "How do you figure that?"

So, they weren't done. She let the box drop again with a smack to the floor. "The first sign things weren't going his way between us, he jumps on a plane and takes a job in Europe. Europe!"

Leah crossed her arms in front of her. "It's not the same."

"It feels the same." Caroline picked up the box again and pushed past Leah. "Only, I refuse to be Mom and chase him across the world, losing bits of my heart all along the way. I'm just glad I found out before I told him how I felt."

Leah followed her down the aisle. "Have you considered that he's only going because he doesn't know how you feel—that unlike Dad—if you asked him to stay, he would?"

Would he?

Ripping the tape off the box, Caroline lifted out a stack of postcards, stood, and started filling the wire carousel. "Until trouble came again and then—"

"Are you listening to yourself? He didn't leave because you two had a fight or because he's got that itch for an adventure. He's leaving because you broke his heart and he can't stay and watch you and Mason plan the life he wants with you."

"That's a stretch."

"Caroline, you didn't see his face when he left. That guy was devastated."

She added a few more postcards and drew a deep breath, forcing her lungs to expand. "He never told me he loved me. He barely hinted that he really liked me. And he sure as anything made it clear that he had no intention of making future plans with me or anyone."

"Would you stop?" Leah grabbed at the cards in Caroline's hand but missed, sending the stack to the floor instead. "First of all, do you expect the guy to be ready to talk marriage before you've even had a third date? Second of all, face it, you aren't the easiest person to be honest with."

Caroline bent down to pick them up. "What does that mean?"

Leah knelt next to her and helped gather the scattered cards. "It means between your lists, plans, and strong opinions about everyone's life, you aren't the easiest person to open up to."

"I'm a life coach. Listening—"

"Should be what you're good at. But the closer people get to you, the less you listen. Once you get a plan in your head, you refuse to let go even when it's failing." Leah slammed a small stack of cards on the box, pulled her knees up, and buried her head in her hands.

"What's this really about?"

Leah lifted her head and stared off into space then locked eyes with Caroline again. "I think we should close the store."

"What?" Caroline sat back and stared at Leah. "I thought this was your dream."

"It was. But we've both seen the books. Face it, that dream is ending, and I think it's time to find a new one. You want to be a life coach, and I want to . . . do anything but shelve night-lights for the rest of my life."

Caroline's gaze shifted to the photo of their grandfather that hung by the door. She couldn't envision a life where her family didn't run the WIFI, but truthfully, she'd always envisioned Leah here. If this wasn't what Leah wanted anymore, then she had no right to wish it upon her.

Caroline closed her eyes as a tear dropped down her cheek. She rested her head back against a shelf. "What'll you do?"

Leah paused as if weighing her next words. "David sent me a letter and asked me to join him."

"In Costa Rica?" Was everyone she loved leaving the country?

"I know you didn't agree with David's decision to go, but—"

"It was a knee-jerk reaction to his breakup with Sadie. The three of us had a plan for the store, and he walked away on a whim. Of course I was going to try and talk him out of it."

Leah shook her head. "He'd talked about going into missions since he was in junior high. He never wanted the store. That was Grandfather's plan and then our plan. Never David's." She sighed and shook her head. "Costa Rica may have come together quickly, but it wasn't a knee-jerk reaction."

Caroline thought back to the days when she was balancing college, the store, and their grandparents' failing health. Had he been trying to tell her?

What had Grant told her once? *A lot of us aren't as good at spilling our guts as others. Our opening up is much more subtle.*

"We aren't abandoning you, Caroline. We're living our lives." Leah nudged Caroline's shoulder with her own. "I think it's time for you to start doing that too. And I think that starts by talking to Grant."

The bell above them chimed as Nate walked in and scanned the room. He found them and lifted one eyebrow. "Everything okay?"

"It will be." Leah gave Caroline a pointed look. "As soon as Caroline goes and talks to Grant."

"He left."

"What?" Both girls sat up straighter.

"I was supposed to take him to the airport, but George Kensington was headed that way, so he took him. Left a few minutes ago. Didn't he tell you he was leaving?"

"Yes, but I didn't realize . . ." Caroline drew in a slow breath, trying to process everything.

"Call him." Leah held out her phone.

Caroline fished out her own phone and tapped his number. It rang three times then went to voicemail. She ended the call and bit back the lump in her throat.

"He's supposed to be back on Wednesday." Nate dropped to the floor next to them, picking up a few postcards that escaped that direction.

Caroline put her phone back into her pocket. "Maybe it's for the best. This isn't really a phone call kind of conversation. It can wait until Wednesday."

Leah leaned toward her. "But, Caroline—"

"No." She locked eyes with her sister. "I know I'm being unfair to say he's like Dad. But the fact remains, he's still running, and I think he's been running since he left the Army. Until he finds what he's looking for, I'm not sure it could ever work between us, anyway."

"I agree." Nate passed the postcards in his hands to Leah. "I love Grant, and I'd love for you two to get together, but right now, he's looking for answers that you can't provide—nor can I."

Leah gathered the postcards that were still on the floor and added them to the box. "He still deserves to know you love him."

"We'll talk . . . after the interview."

Leah stared at her, her lips pressed into a thin line.

"I promise." That was the plan anyway, but she was slowly learning that plans had a way of not coming together.

thirteen

Are you running toward something or away from something?

George's question from the ride here played on repeat in Grant's brain. It hadn't helped that it was pretty much what Nate had said to him too. He hadn't had an answer for George, and he still didn't have one now.

He leaned against the floor-to-ceiling window as a plane took flight in the distance. An angled conveyor belt emptied suitcase after suitcase off the plane he was waiting to board, while a man with headphones and orange sticks directed another plane to park.

Grant glanced at his phone again and the missed call from Caroline. He hadn't really missed it, but the phone didn't make a separate category for declined calls.

For a person who values honesty so much—you're really *bad at it.*

Caroline was right. He was so bad at honesty that he couldn't even seem to be honest with himself. Did he love her?

Love was a huge step. But the way his heart had scraped across gravel at the sight of that ring, maybe he *was* in love—or not far off. But it didn't matter, because what woman kept the ring unless she was at least giving it consideration?

But then she'd called. Grant pulled out his phone and stared at her name in his list of contacts—his finger hovering over her name.

His phone rang in his hand. Unknown number.

"Hello."

"Quinn! Tell me it's true."

"Conway?"

"Who else, dipwad? Now tell me when you're getting here." Justin Conway had been on his team a few years back. The guy had a colorful mouth but at least he was keeping it PG today. But fewer guys had a truer heart. He'd been there for Quinn when he'd gotten his Dear John letter from Emily and the day Quinn had woken up with his life changed by the explosion.

"I'm getting on the plane in a few minutes." *At least I think I am.*

"I about messed myself when I heard. It'll be great getting the team back together. Jackson's here too."

Team.

His team. His life had many pieces he couldn't fit together right now. But a team—that he could figure out.

"You can stay with Coop and me until you get a place. What time are you getting in? I'll pick you up."

This was it. Was he going or not?

His team needed him and Caroline said she didn't.

"Sir." A woman in a blue suit stood before him. "Sir, are you a ticketed passenger? This is the final boarding."

"I get in at ten-fifteen. See ya then."

Grant powered down his phone and shoved it into his pocket. He boarded the plane and followed the flow of people to 25B. He offered an apology to the person on the aisle as he squished past. Last-minute ticket meant the middle seat. Awesome.

The girl by the window leaned over a notebook with different colored sticky notes lined up across the top while she studied a small stack of flash cards. Her handwriting was neat and tight, and she had the scientific name of a different body part on each card. Maybe she was studying biology. Or how to dismember people.

She leaned over to dig through her bag. Her red hair was nearly the same shade as Caroline's but longer. More like it had been back when Caroline had been eighteen.

Grant looked away. He didn't want to think about Caroline right now.

He reached in his pack for the candy bar he'd purchased in the airport, but his hand found a book. He pulled out his Bible and stared at the cover held together at the spine by duct tape. He hadn't packed his Bible. Nate. The guy just wouldn't give up.

Grant thumbed through a few pages. How many hours had he spent studying these pages before . . . before everything had fallen apart? The page fell open to where a well-worn envelope had been tucked. Caroline's last letter to him.

He pulled the letter from the envelope and smoothed it out.

Dear Grant,

Since I have never heard back from you, I assume either you have been deployed where there's no communication—like the deepest regions of the rain forest or the top of Mount Everest—or you don't ever plan on writing back.

I probably shouldn't write this final letter—just let it end naturally. But I feel in all the things I said to you there's one thing I never had the guts to say.

It is okay to let people in. I know you're strong and you like to be strong for those around you. But being vulnerable isn't a weakness. It is a strength.

I hope you have found someone who you can let in.

Caroline

P.S. Goodbye.

How would things have turned out if he'd answered this one letter—or any of them?

But the truth was he hadn't known what to say then and he still didn't. He hadn't let Emily in, and when he'd tried to let Caroline in, she'd pushed him away. No, that wasn't fair. He'd never really let her in either. He'd only let her in the safe areas. The areas where he'd mostly healed. He had shown her his scars, but he hadn't come close to showing her his open wounds.

He turned to the girl next to him. "Could I use a piece of your paper?"

The girl tore off a piece and held it up, her focus still on one of her note cards.

"Thanks." He felt in his backpack for a pen but came up with nothing.

The girl held up a blue pen as she flipped another flashcard.

"Thanks."

Where did he start? Maybe it wasn't *what* he said but the fact that he was willing to say it. To open up and share a piece of who he was in each letter. He'd start by addressing the last thing she'd written in that letter long ago.

Dear Caroline,

I'm not ready to say goodbye . . .

Who knew that five days could pass so slowly? Caroline stared at the front of Nate's house, Grant's bike, and finally Nate's car. With all vehicles accounted for, Grant had to be inside. She'd just expected—hoped—that Grant would've called her when he got back in town. But it had been over twenty-four hours and still nothing. She wasn't letting him leave town again without talking to him.

Caroline got out of her car and made her way to the front porch. She knocked once and then again with more force. Nate's distant voice came through the door. "Come in."

The kitchen was empty. Just a table piled with boxes. "Hello?"

Nate entered with another box in his arms and dropped it on the table with the others. "Hey. What's up?"

"Is Grant around?" She ducked her head and started stacking the boxes with the largest on the bottom. Anything to keep her hands busy. "I thought you'd already unpacked."

"Sorry. I thought he called you."

Caroline paused with a box in midair. "What?"

Nate winced and shook his head. "He decided to take the job. He's . . . not coming back."

She focused on the box in her hands and then the others. Each one was addressed to Grant Quinn in Florida. "What about his bike?"

"He sold it to me."

Her legs went weak and she dropped into a chair.

Breathe. In. Out. In. Out.

He'd never sell his bike unless he really wasn't returning.

Nate squatted down in her vision. "I'm so sorry. I should've never encouraged you. Grant has a lot he needs to work through. I thought . . . I'd hoped . . ." He released a deep sigh before standing. "I'm sorry."

He pulled her to her feet and wrapped her in a huge hug. Tears formed in her eyes as a sob clogged her throat. She swallowed it back.

After a minute, he leaned away. "What will you do now that the WIFI is closing?"

"I don't know." She wiped the tears on her face. "Seems everything I plan falls apart."

"What about your life coaching business?" He pulled two or three Kleenexes from a tissue box and held them out. "You've got some savings to live off for a bit, and I think if you really invested some time into it, it could take off."

She accepted the tissues and dabbed her face again. "And if it doesn't? I'll have eaten through my savings and still have nothing."

"It's okay to fail sometimes." Nate pulled out a chair from the kitchen table and sat down and then pointed to the other. "God can work with that."

Caroline plopped in the opposite chair. "I don't *want* to fail."

"No one does." He drummed his fingers on the table. "I'm not asking you to fail. I'm saying you need to step out and live the life God's called you to—really live that dream—without a backup plan."

"But that's . . . terrifying." Caroline stood again and paced a few feet away.

"Life is scary sometimes and that's okay. Relationships are scary sometimes. But if you never put yourself out there, you won't find love and you'll never really live."

"My mom put it out there again and again, and it never worked out for her."

Nate nudged the chair and waited until she sat again. He leaned toward her, propping his elbows on his knees. "I don't know all the details about your parents' marriage, and I'm guessing if you're honest with yourself, you don't really either. I do know that you can't be afraid your whole life based on what you saw your mom go through."

"I'm not afraid." The words tasted like a lie. She'd been afraid to be honest with Grant. And afraid that it was more than just her list that was wrong. If her whole life approach was wrong, then everything she'd worked toward over the past five years had been a waste. "I'm applying what I learned from her and I'm choosing a different way."

"A safe way. A way that—at this rate—means you'll never quite reach your dream."

"That's unfair." Caroline stood and filled a glass with water.

"I'm not trying to make you mad, Caroline. But you'll never reach the dream if you don't trust God to get you there."

She leaned against the counter and downed a few swallows. "So, I should throw away all my plans, like Grant did?"

"I don't know. But I know Someone who does."

"Right. God." She couldn't keep the sarcasm from her voice as she set the glass in the sink with more force than necessary.

"When I first felt called to be a pastor, I thought God would call me to the streets of Detroit. But He didn't. He put me here. Could you get farther from the streets of Detroit than Heritage? This isn't what I thought I was saying yes to. But the truth is, I didn't say yes to pastoring in the inner city. I said yes to serving God where He put me, and believe it or not, He put me here. To be honest—I'm still not sure all the people of this town agree with Him. I just have to trust He has a plan, and my job is to wake up and say yes to that plan every day."

"People here love you."

"Not all of them. But that isn't the point. Remember, God promises to direct our paths when we submit to Him. He doesn't promise to bless any plan we decide on our own to make. We get that confused sometimes."

Caroline sat in the chair once again. Is that what she was doing? Yes, because when she thought about the times she'd prayed, she rarely waited for an answer. She didn't even know what God's answer would sound like.

Nate came and stood in front of her. "I'm not trying to give you a sermon."

"Yet, you're succeeding." She lifted one eyebrow at him.

He laughed as he pulled her to her feet and into another hug. "I care about you. And I believe God has so much more for you. But you have to be willing to follow."

"Something to think about." She nodded and turned toward the door. She needed to get away before she started blubbering all over him again. "I'll see you later."

"I'm counting on it."

Outside, Caroline paused before unlocking her car and stared at Grant's bike. No, not Grant's anymore. The pain scraped fresh again. He wasn't returning.

She'd been leading the charge since her mother passed, determined not to end up like her. She hadn't turned out like her mom, that was for certain, and yet she'd ended up with the same fate. Left behind.

Her plans were meant to keep this from happening, but they hadn't.

Sliding into her car, she laid her head against the steering wheel as tears began to flow. She couldn't even form a prayer with her words, the pain was too intense. The pain of losing Grant. The pain of trying to be the one to hold the family together since her mom passed. The pain of having nothing left. Could God work with nothing? That was what her grandma had always told her, but did she really believe that?

Okay, God. Now what?

It wasn't the most eloquent prayer she'd ever uttered, but it was all she had. She stayed with her forehead resting on the steering wheel. Waiting. She wasn't even sure what she was waiting for.

After more than fifteen minutes, she still didn't have a plan, but one thing she did feel certain about—she still had to be honest with Grant.

He'd made his decision. But she couldn't get away from the feeling that—whether for her benefit or his—it was time to lay it all out there. It was time to write him one more letter.

fourteen

Why had he ever decided to sell his motorcycle? Grant turned down an empty road and opened up the throttle on Cooper's Harley. The wind rushed past him, stripping away the tightness that pulled at his chest, but it still didn't erase the itch under his skin. The month he'd spent here in Florida for training was going great—so why did he feel like this? The green on-ramp sign to I-75 grew in the distance. Maybe he should drive north. North to Michigan. His ranch. Anywhere but here.

Run away again.

Caroline was right. As soon as something wasn't sitting right, his first instinct was to bolt. No, more than instinct. A compulsive need that nearly strangled the air from his lungs.

He'd done his best to keep Caroline and her parting words out of his thoughts over the past month, but occasionally, she slid under his defenses. He'd never missed Emily like this. He'd never missed anyone like this.

Why couldn't he see anything through?

Not even the ending of his relationship with Caroline. Her letter had arrived a month ago. Yet it still remained in his leather coat pocket unopened for the same reason he hadn't mailed the letter he'd written on the plane or any of the dozen that he'd written since then.

Whether she wanted him back or not, he wasn't sure he was ready for either. If she no longer wanted him . . . the idea was too much to think about.

But if she wanted him back, he couldn't do that either. After all, how could he be who she needed him to be if he couldn't stay in one place for very long? He'd always be running, and that wasn't fair to her.

He'd heard it said that no one can outrun God. But he'd sure tried.

A dark line across the road appeared in the distance. He downshifted and slowed the bike. A black cable stretched from one side to the other. Not even big enough to cause much of a bump.

A cable.

He stopped the bike five yards back from it as a cold chill traveled down his arms and into his hands. What was wrong with him?

It was *just* a cable.

His lungs struggled to find enough air.

Just a cable.

No matter what he told his brain, he couldn't drive over it.

Grant pulled the motorcycle to the side of the road, dropped the kickstand, and slid off, falling to his knees. The gravel bit into his skin through his jeans as darkness gathered at the edges of his vision.

Why wasn't there enough air?

He closed his eyes and drew in a slow breath. It didn't help. Screams echoed from far away as burning pain radiated down his face.

He tried to force his eyes open, but the world was too bright, too much.

That blasted cable.

Grant rolled onto his back and focused on breathing. In through his nose, out through his mouth. In. Out.

So many people wanted to be on his team and he'd pushed them away. Over and over. And now he was going to die. Right here on the side of the road. Alone. "Lord, help me."

In. Out.

His phone rang in his pocket. He ignored it. In. Out.

The gravel near him crunched, followed by a slamming door. "Son, are you okay? Do you need me to call someone?"

Son. The word echoed around in his head. Son.

"Dad?" Grant forced his eyes open. The man leaning over him wasn't his father, but he had a kind face and was saying something. No, he was trying to get Grant to sit up. He looked like . . .

"George?" Grant took the offered hand. And then the water bottle the man was holding out.

"No. The name's Walt. Can I call someone? Do you know what happened?" The man knelt next to Grant.

Grant blinked some clarity back into his head. "I think I had a panic attack."

The man brushed his silvery hair back and sat on the grass next to Grant. "Has this ever happened before?"

"Never this bad." Grant rested his elbows on his knees and drew a long swig of the water. Then pointed to the cable. "I couldn't drive over it." Grant rubbed his hand over the scar.

"Did you serve in the war?"

"Yeah."

"Have you ever considered getting help?"

"I didn't think . . . It's never been . . ."

"Untreated PTSD can become worse. After the Vietnam War, many of my buddies . . . they didn't do well. But there are many options today." The man reached into his wallet and pulled out a card. "I keep this in here for times like this."

Grant accepted the card.

VA Hotline.

Maybe it was time to stop doing this on his own. "Thanks."

"Do you need me to help you get somewhere?" Walt pushed to his feet.

"I'm going to sit a few minutes. Then I'll drive back."

Walt studied him.

"I'll be okay. Really."

The man nodded and returned to his car.

What were the chances that a man with a VA card in his pocket would be the one to stop and help him? Probably pretty good since the last words he'd muttered were *Lord, help me*. God had shown up. At this point, Grant wouldn't even have been surprised to find out the guy was an angel.

Grant dropped his head in his hands. It was time to stop blaming God. God was with him, not against him. Always had been. Right here on the side of the road in his panic attack and back in the Humvee when the IED had ripped apart his life. He'd never left him.

Grant put the card inside the pocket of his leather coat, his fingers brushing across a familiar envelope. It was time.

Grant pulled it out and tore the seal.

Grant,

You once said that you loved it when I was honest in my letters. Well, here I am, and I'll be as honest as I can.

I love you.

I know I should say those words for the first time out loud, but I figured if I'm going to be honest here, then I wouldn't hold anything back.

I said no to Mason. I should have told you that when you were in my office. I told him no right away. Not because the guy cheated on me with Melissa (although I would've said no for that). I said no because I realized that he wasn't the man I wanted at all. My list was wrong. Dead wrong.

I'm sorry I didn't tell you. I was mad, scared, confused, and probably many other emotions I can't even think of right now. When you walked away, it was like watching my father walk away all those years ago. I took out years of anger and hurt on you without giving you a chance. I'm sorry.

I don't know what comes next for us. I don't even know if you'll write back. But I've discovered something. I don't need a plan with you. I'm done making plans. I just want you.

With all my heart.

Love, Caroline

Grant didn't know what he wanted to do with the rest of his life, but he did know two things. He needed help and he wanted Caroline.

George's words came back to him. *Are you running toward something or away from something?* Grant had spent much of his life running away from things. Maybe it was time to run toward some things.

Who knew that letting go of a plan took so much . . . well . . . planning? Caroline crossed off the last item on her list. The WIFI was now officially a part of Heritage's past. She dropped her calendar in the final box and gazed around the empty store. Everything was gone. Even the shelving had been sold off.

George Kensington had given them a fair price for their half of the building even though his own half still stood empty. He'd even given them a three-year out clause. If Caroline or Leah decided in those three years that they wanted to open a business—any business—again, they could buy it back at the same price—which seemed overly generous. But since the town was full of more empty buildings than occupied ones, Caroline thought that he did it in hopes that they'd change their minds.

Caroline didn't see changing her mind. She wasn't completely sure where she was headed next, but retail wasn't one of the options. She'd had another call about her life coaching business the other day. That made three clients. Not enough to live on but enough to keep her busy while shutting down the store.

Leah had been a lot of help, but she'd also been spending hours ironing out the details for Costa Rica. She'd never seen Leah this motivated about anything.

Caroline picked up the last box, gave the store one last look, and pulled the door open a final time. The familiar jingle paused her steps. She'd loved that sound as a child and the memories it still brought her every day—the smell, Grandfather's smile, her grandmother sneaking her candy from the glass jar.

Caroline unhooked the bell from above the door and added it to the box on her hip.

She pulled the door shut and turned the key on her past—and the hope of a new future.

"Leave town for a few weeks and the whole place shuts down."

Caroline spun toward Grant's voice and almost lost hold of the box. "You're here."

That was brilliant. Of course he was here. Here in his leather jacket and a snug gray T-shirt that boasted ARMY across his chest. The scruff that had darkened his chin before had been shaved clean and close. His hair was neatly trimmed but still longer than military regulations. He seemed lighter and happier than she remembered him.

"It looks like the new job has been good to you."

He shrugged and offered her a teasing smile. "You trying to say I look good?"

If he was only here for a stopover, she was in trouble.

"Why are you here?" The words came out breathy.

Had he received her letter?

He held up a key. "Take a ride with me."

A ride? By the size of that key, he wasn't talking Nate's car.

"I thought you sold it."

He cringed. "I did. But Nate let me borrow it. This has to be a record temperature for November, and I couldn't waste it in a car."

This was it. Was she really going to trust him? Not just with her heart, but her life?

"I brought you your own helmet and everything." He held up a pink helmet and waited.

Her hesitation must have shown on her face because he added, "Or we can walk."

"No."

"No?" The smile on his face disappeared as he lowered the helmet.

"No, I mean I wouldn't rather walk. I'll ride." She held her breath. Just thinking about getting on that bike made her dizzy. But as that heart-stopping smile that she'd grown to love filled Grant's face, she had no doubt that she'd made the right decision.

"Let me just put this box in my car." Caroline walked to her car and dropped the box in the trunk.

"Otis finally made his way to your store."

Caroline shut the trunk and stared at the brass animal. "Yup, he showed up shortly after we announced we were closing. Like he came to say goodbye. In his own way, he made the end less painful." She stepped closer and knelt to rub his shiny brass nose. "Thank you, Otis."

Grant stood next to his motorcycle just watching her. She had so many questions, but she needed to go with the flow on this. He settled the pink helmet on her head, tucked her hair back, and tightened the buckle. His gentle touch had every inch of her on alert.

He reached for his own helmet and climbed onto the Harley before he guided her on, pointing out where to sit, where to put her feet, and how to hold on. It was probably best that he'd left that last instruction until the end since every coherent thought flew out of her head as she wrapped her arms around his waist.

She buried her face in his back as the motorcycle moved forward. Drawing in a deep breath of his scent, she shoved away the reality that they were traveling unprotected at high speeds, where death could find them at any minute.

"Look up." Grant's voice vibrated his chest, and she was pretty sure she only heard him because her ear was pressed against his back. She held on tighter.

"Look up. Just once."

Caroline squeezed tighter, lifted her head, and forced her eyes open. Trees clinging to the tail end of fall made a canopy over the road, their branches intertwined as shafts of mid-day light peeked through to the road below. Wow. Her breath left her. Had there ever been a more perfect moment?

Grant wasn't racing down the street. He wasn't even going fast—introducing her to something new, but being gentle with her at the same time. Caroline tilted her head back and let the breeze wash over her. No doubt her hair would be a mess of tangles when this was over, but she didn't care. She could stay like this all day.

A car came over the hill the opposite way, so close it seemed as if she could have reached out and touched it. She squeezed Grant around the chest tighter and buried her head once more.

Grant's chuckle shook his chest. The bike slowed and leaned. They must have turned off the main road, but she refused to look up again.

When they finally stopped, she loosened her grip and opened

her eyes. "Little Sable. I used to come here with my grandparents a lot when I was a kid. I love this place. I'd still spend every free minute of my summer here if it hadn't become such a vacation spot for out-of-towners."

Grant helped her off and stashed their helmets before turning them down the path. They stopped at the base of the lighthouse. The deep red brick contrasted against the deep blue autumn sky.

Grant patted the brick a few times before he turned his gaze toward the water's edge. "I left the interview because there were no windows. I don't do well without windows."

"Because of the accident?"

He nodded as he took a few steps toward the water. "I was in the back of a Humvee when the driver hit an IED. Not that I could've done better if I'd been the driver. But not being able to see . . . It messes with your head."

"So do you have PTSD?"

Grant's shoulders stiffened. "Yes. I still haven't grown used to the label, but I've been seeing someone and they've been helping me."

"It takes a strong man to ask for help."

"That's what I'm learning." His hand brushed a wisp of hair behind her ear, his finger lingering on the side of her face.

"Is that why you're back? To get help?"

"Partly, but I'm also back because of this." Grant reached into his pocket and pulled out her letter. "It has been a long time since someone was this honest with me, and I must say it was nice."

"Nice?"

"Better than nice." He unfolded the letter. "But there are a couple parts I don't agree with."

"Wait, you've come to debate my letter?"

"Yes. Like when you say here, 'I'm done making plans.'" He glanced up but still held the note between them. "You can't quit making plans."

"But my plans—"

"You're one of the most gifted planners I know. That's how God made you. Don't give that up. But don't let it limit you either."

His words lifted a weight that had been pressing on her since her talk with Leah. Maybe she wasn't failing at life. She just needed to allow some flexibility.

"I was wrong to think I could live without a plan. Face it, my heart is military, and one thing the military does is make plans. I just have to remember—"

"'No plan survives contact with the enemy.'"

"Exactly. And I've learned that I'm not in this alone."

"You mean God?"

"I'm slowly finding my way back to Him, but I also mean you. I want you on my team." He reached in his leather jacket and pulled out a stack of envelopes bound by a rubber band. "I told you once that if I ever wrote you one letter, I'd never be able to stop. Turns out I was right. I know I'm a work in progress, but this is a little bit of me just for you."

Caroline swallowed and took the stack of envelopes.

"You also said in your letter, 'I don't need a plan with you.'" Grant wrapped his free arm around her and pulled her close. "That's a problem. I *want* to make plans with you."

Caroline bit her lip. "I did make one more list."

His eyebrows lifted. "What list is that?"

"A new perfect-guy list." Caroline pulled a paper out of her back pocket and unfolded it.

"At least it's shorter this time." Grant laughed, but his eyes held a touch of uncertainty.

"Very short. Just two items on the list."

"Two?"

"Yup. It's pretty simple actually: Loves God. Loves me." She folded the paper and slid it back into her pocket. "That's it. The rest of the details we'll work out along the way."

"I like that list." Grant closed what little space remained between them. He lowered his mouth to hers, soft at first. Testing and teasing the edges of her lips. Caroline closed her eyes and leaned in to his touch as a slight whimper escaped.

That seemed to be all the encouragement Grant needed. The paper in his hand wrinkled as he grabbed the sides of her shirt and pressed her back against the side of the lighthouse deepening the kiss. His right hand captured her jaw a moment then left a trail of fire as it moved to her neck.

He smelled like wind and tasted like adventure. It was alarming and reassuring at the same time. Who knew where life would take them? But she trusted Grant.

When Grant finally pulled back, both breathed with a little more effort and Caroline had to resist the urge to pull him back in for more. Yearning didn't seem like a strong enough word.

"I love you, Caroline." His voice came out husky. "I love everything about you, even your list making and minute-by-minute scheduled ways. I want you. And I do want to make plans with you."

"So what about the job in Europe? We can make it work. We can—"

"No."

"No what?"

"After talking to a life coach, I realized I need to pursue something I feel passionate about."

"Sounds like a smart lady." Her fingers trailed the edge of his shirt. "So, what would that be?"

"Turning my ranch into a place for at-risk teens." His thumb found the skin at her lower back and trailed a small circle as he talked.

"Really?"

"Yup. Know anyone who's good at turning an idea into a plan?"

She tapped her chin with her index finger. "I just might."

"Do you need to get back to your to-do list for the day?"

"Nope. The day is yours."

Grant folded her letter and returned it to his pocket. "What do you want to do?"

She hooked her finger through one of his belt loops and tugged him closer. "Surprise me."

What Happens Next?

Read the first chapter of Book One in the Restoring Heritage Series

You Belong with Me

chapter one

Was she really the only one left who cared about this town?

Hannah Thornton shivered as a chill traveled over her skin. Her '76 Volkswagen Bug might be a classic, but it didn't offer much protection from the icy chill of February in Michigan. The streetlight highlighted a few scattered snowflakes that drifted down from the dark sky. Cold or not, she loved winter and all its beauty.

Hannah popped open the car door and paused. Gray slush merged with a murky pothole just outside her door. Ugh. Winter was also this.

Stretching her long leg out, Hannah attempted to hurtle the mess, but the icy stream that filled her new pink pumps testified to her failure and stole her breath. With a slam of her door, Hannah turned toward the sidewalk and then hobbled over to Otis, the town's brass hippo. She dusted off his wide, brown back and sat. "Thanks, Otis. You have a knack for being right where we need you."

"Hannah—wait. I need to talk to you." Her brother, Thomas, slammed his front door a few yards away then hurried down the porch toward her. "I thought you had a house showing tonight."

"I did. Or tried to. But only Dale Kensington showed up."

"Sorry."

"I don't want to talk about it." She shook the slush from her shoe. "Why wouldn't someone want to live in Heritage? We are halfway between Ludington and Muskegon and a stone's throw from Lake Michigan. It's a summer vacation dream."

"You have to admit, it's seen better days."

"Heritage is full of history—ours and other people's. Maybe the sidewalks are cracked and the roads need repaired, but they're the same sidewalks we played hopscotch on as kids and the same roads we learned to ride our bikes on." It was home—an anchor no matter what life threw at you. Hannah pushed back her emotions as she tapped the side of the brass animal. "And we have our likable quirks—like our wandering hippo."

"Why are you sitting on Otis when it's thirty degrees out?" His breath created white puffs with every word.

"Fixing my shoe." She waved the pink pump at him. "And I came to vent to Luke." Hannah motioned to the old Victorian in front of her. The windows were dark but Luke was home. He was always home. Her constant.

One of Thomas's eyebrows lifted.

"Stop it. He's my best friend."

"Friend?"

Her focus snapped to his piercing blue eyes, so much like Dad's. Totally unfair—while she had to see Mom's dark hair and murky hazel eyes in the mirror.

Hannah slid her shoe back on and stood. "Yes. Luke is my *friend*."

"Whatever. There's something I need to tell you." Thomas shifted from one stocking foot to the other on the freezing cement. Where were his shoes?

"Thomas?" The door of his house slammed again as his girlfriend, Madison Westmore, emerged, hugging her too-tan-for-February bare arms. "What are you doing out here? I have to go home soon."

His shoulders stiffened. "I'll be right—"

"Hannah?" Her sweet tone—no doubt for Thomas's benefit—fell flat. No love lost on either side. What did he see in her?

Madison closed the distance to Thomas, gripping his arm as if to claim his warmth. "Did you tell her?"

A look of panic crossed Thomas's face. "I was about—"

"We're engaged." Madison thrust her hand forward.

Hannah blinked several times then darted a glance at her older brother. "Wow. That's . . . wow."

How could he be marrying her? He should be marrying Janie. Kind, wonderful Janie, who was coming home from Europe in a few days. This was going to devastate her.

Hannah clenched her teeth and forced her face into what she hoped looked like a smile. "Congratulations. When's the big day?"

Madison tossed her bottle-blonde hair over her shoulder. "It depends on how long it takes to sell this dump."

Hannah's mouth dropped open as a sudden coldness far more intense than the icy bite of Michigan winter spread through her core. Madison did not just call the house her great-grandfather had designed and built a dump.

"Hannah." Thomas's voice held a desperate edge. His arm dropped on her shoulder before he faced Madison. "You look cold. Why don't you go back in? I'll be just a minute."

Madison eyed him a moment and then dropped a kiss on his cheek. "Fine."

Hannah swallowed the avalanche of words that sprung to mind as Madison and her miniskirt disappeared into his house.

Thomas squeezed her around the shoulders, sharing a bit of warmth as he rested his chin on her head. "I was trying to tell you. I hadn't even planned on proposing so soon. It just . . ."

Her hands flew into the air and she stepped away. "Not planned? She has the ring. Wait, why didn't you use Grandma Hazel's ring?"

He stared up at the stars before focusing back on her. "I'll tell you everything, but not tonight. Tonight I need you to be happy for me, bug."

Hannah inhaled a lungful of frigid air and let it out, slow and controlled. Pulling out the childhood nicknames? So unfair. "I will be. I . . . am. Just don't sell the house."

Thomas rubbed his arms as he glanced back at his place—the place she'd grown up in. "Madison wants you to list it this week."

She bit her cheek until the coppery taste of blood filled her mouth. "I'll buy it."

"I'd love for you to have it, but after buying your half last year I can't afford to give it to you." He shook his head and crossed his arms in front of him, shifting his feet again. "From what I remember, you put all that money into paying off student loans and your Realtor business. So what happened tonight? I thought Kensington wanted that property."

"He wants to tear that sweet little house down." She shifted her gaze from her brother to the stars when her voice wavered. "I'll convince the Fergusons to wait for another buyer."

"You think that's wise?"

"No." Why had she ever thought she could be a Realtor? Why had she let Thomas buy her half of the house? Because she thought he'd planned on marrying Janie and raising a family there—not selling it and marrying *Madison.*

Looks like she'd been wrong. Maybe she'd been wrong about a lot.

"I've got to go." Her breath fogged in the cold air.

"Think about it. We're selling it—like it or not." He shrugged as he stepped toward the house. "At least this way you'd get the commission."

The wind nipped at her cheeks as she hurried to Luke's side door as fast as her heels would let her. She banged on the screen door and waited as the kitchen light flicked on. The door stuck, then creaked open. Luke leaned against the doorjamb in jeans and a white T-shirt, backlit by the kitchen.

A scattering of drywall dust highlighted his short brown curls as they escaped in a reckless mess around his head. The five-o'clock shadow and the tool belt that hung low on his hips confirmed that he didn't have any big plans. She couldn't see his brown eyes in the shadows, but they were as familiar as her morning cup of coffee. He crossed his arms over his broad chest, pulling his shirt snug across his shoulders.

"Hannah, Hannah, Hannah." That endearing dimple formed in his left cheek. If she hadn't wanted to slap the smug expression off his face, she might have been tempted to kiss it. Best friends really shouldn't be allowed to be that good-looking. Besides, she knew better than to kiss Luke. Again.

She pushed past him into the house. "Don't say it!"

No way did she want to hear whatever was behind that grin right now. She needed comfort. She needed an escape. She needed ice cream.

Hannah claimed her regular spot at the kitchen table, the same table where she'd been finding comfort since elementary school.

Only then, the house had smelled of coffee and homemade chocolate chip cookies. The aroma of coffee remained, but now it mingled with the lingering scent of leftover pizza.

Luke pulled a half gallon of chocolate ice cream from the freezer and set it before her.

She stared at the offered gift. "How did you . . . ?"

A smile tilted his lips. No, a smirk. After setting a spoon and a bowl on the table next to the carton, he crossed his arms again and lifted one eyebrow. "Everyone knows Kensington wants that land—not the house. I don't know why you thought you could talk him into anything else. Did anyone else show?"

"No." Hannah peeled the lid off the ice cream with a sigh. "I have to convince them not to sell to him."

"You're the only Realtor I know who actually tries to talk people out of selling and buying. Might be time for a different job."

Hannah jabbed her spoon into the ice cream and started to carve out a ball. "I help them understand the history they're throwing away. Or in this case, wanting to destroy in the name of progress." She dropped the scoop in the dish and lifted her chin. "But I *can* be a Realtor."

"Really? You could sell a house to Kensington, or any other developer, if that's what the owner chose?"

"It's possible."

"Were you even able to finish the meeting tonight without losing your temper?"

Hannah worked at forming another ball with her spoon. "I may have emphasized my position with volume at one point."

"I'm guessing it was more like . . ." Luke made the sound of an explosion as he lifted his hands in the air.

Ugh! She whipped her spoon at him.

He ducked and laughed as it clanged against the stove. "What was that for? Honesty?"

She bit back the smile that tugged at the corner of her mouth. She may have overreacted a bit in the meeting. "Yes. Sometimes I'd rather you lie to me. As one of my best friends, your job is simply to feed me ice cream and tell me I'm pretty."

"You're pretty."

Did he have to sound so sarcastic when he said it? She focused back on the ice cream. Shoot. Now she didn't have a spoon.

"I'm simply passionate about preserving history." She stood, grabbed another utensil, and then bumped the drawer closed with a smack of her hip. "My great-great-great-grandfather—"

"—helped found the town. I've heard. But this town is full of houses with history, and from what I can tell, the Kensington family has plans."

"Yeah, well, I hate their plans. More than that, I think George Kensington would hate their plans. *He* loved this town. If he was here to see what his brother was doing with his company, it'd break his heart." Hannah dropped a final scoop in her bowl, then returned the lid to the carton.

This subject was going to give her a migraine. Then there was her brother.

She returned the ice cream to the freezer and slammed the door. "Here's a news flash. Thomas proposed to Madison."

"What? They've been dating—"

"A few months. *Only* a few months." She squeezed her spoon, the metal pressing into her palm. "What does he see in her, anyway?"

"Well . . ." Luke leaned against the counter, lips twisted as he wrinkled his forehead.

"Do guys only think of one thing?" She popped him on the forehead with her fingers. "They've got nothing in common."

He pulled a Coke from the fridge and cracked it open without looking back. "I seem to remember a day you thought differences didn't matter."

She paused with the spoon halfway to her mouth as warmth washed over her face. Oh no he didn't. She popped the spoonful of ice cream into her mouth, letting the sweet cream cool her from the inside.

She'd never let on how much he'd hurt her that day, and she wasn't about to change that. She forced a smile and hoped it looked casual. "Good thing you were there to set me straight."

He took a sip and studied her. "Maybe things are different now. People change, you know?"

She squirmed under his gaze, the intensity of it burning a dangerous path into memories better forgotten. No. She had to be reading too much into it. After seven years of radio silence on the subject, he wouldn't bring it up now. "You mean Madison?"

His Adam's apple bobbed before he looked away and cleared his throat. "Maybe she's different. A lot of people make mistakes in high school."

"Maybe." Were they talking about Madison? Or her? Or him? The boy could give lessons to the military on being cryptic. Didn't matter. Having her heart stomped on once in a lifetime was quite enough. She had the unworn prom dress to prove it.

She scraped the last of her ice cream out of her bowl. Empty already?

Luke crushed his pop can and pitched it in the recycle bin. "Whether she's changed or not, it's not your choice who your brother marries. What's really bugging you?"

"It *is* my business. Who he marries impacts the family. She's already—" Her fingers massaged at the pain building in her temple. "Thomas wants to put our—I mean his house on the market."

"Ah." Luke paused and stared at her.

She blinked faster to keep the tears back. No crying. Luke opened his mouth as if to say something but shut it again. He pulled the carton of ice cream back out of the freezer, peeled off the lid, and slid the whole thing to her.

He was too good to her. Hannah dipped out a spoonful. "First Caroline and Leah left me—"

Luke slid into the chair across from her. "They didn't leave *you*. They closed the WIFI. Caroline got married and Leah became a missionary in Costa Rica. Even you can't complain about that."

"Fine. They had good reasons to leave, but the fact remains that two of my best friends are no longer here. And now Thomas. You don't know how glad I was when you bought this house, even if you're making more changes than I'd like. At least you're sticking around."

Nothing.

Hannah's focus snapped to his unreadable expression. "You are staying in Heritage, right?"

Luke rubbed the back of his neck as he picked at the wood grain of the table. "I better get back to pulling that bathroom sink out."

"Luke?"

He didn't look at her as he stood. "Is it getting cold in here? I better check that fire first."

"Luke."

He disappeared into the living room without looking back. He had to be joking. If Luke left it would be worse than losing Caroline and Leah. Worse than Thomas.

Hannah gripped the edge of the table to steady herself. Heritage without Luke wasn't something she was willing to consider.

Could he settle in Heritage? That was the million-dollar question. Or at least the one that plagued him on sleepless nights. Luke stalked to the fireplace, grabbed another log, and pitched it on the flames. The air shifted and smoke filled his throat. He coughed but didn't turn away. Warmth flooded his face, either from the fire or from the rise in his blood pressure.

What would it take for this place to feel like home—like he belonged?

The faded flowery wallpaper and pink shag carpet weren't much to look at now, but this place was his. He was no longer a kid who had nothing to his name. He was a person of property.

But a home? How would a person who grew up in foster care know about that? A home took more than two-by-fours and drywall. But what exactly it took, he wasn't sure.

In the kitchen, the freezer door clicked shut.

Luke forced a whistle through his lips and returned to where he'd been working in the downstairs bathroom. Renovations were one thing he could figure out. He'd already torn down one of the plaster walls, but the sink needed to be pulled out before he could get to the next one. He popped the buckle on his tool belt, dropped it in a five-gallon pail, and knelt down to inspect the bottom of the molded porcelain.

Hannah stepped up behind him. "Wow, you're . . . making a mess."

"Yup." He glanced at her over his shoulder. Her long dark hair framed her face, highlighting her hazel eyes. Only Hannah could pull off the carefree appearance of a fifteen-year-old and yet still look twenty-five.

"Please tell me you aren't destroying history, worry-whistle man."

Luke twisted his neck to get a better look at how the old fixture attached to the wall. "What did you call me?"

"You whistle that obscure tune when you're upset. You don't even realize it, do you?" She sighed and sat on an overturned bucket in the doorway. "You didn't answer me. Are you destroying history?"

"I don't have a worry-whistle, and some history needs destroyed—replaced, anyway. These plaster walls for starters. Not to mention this knob-and-tube wiring, which stopped being standard in the thirties."

"You do have a worry-whistle, and history needs restored, not destroyed. Plaster is classic and I love the thirties."

He'd let the whistle argument go. "It's a bathroom. The walls need greenboard to handle the moisture. And I'm not keeping the wiring even if you love the history of it. If the crazy splice job some electrician did years back wasn't enough of a reason, the rubber insulation is degrading to the point that it's a fire hazard. But thanks for the suggestion." He worked the bolt to see if it was loose. Nope. "Can you hand me the Crescent wrench?"

A cool metal tool dropped in his hand. He glanced down to adjust it. "This is an open-end wrench."

She sighed, snatched back the tool, and returned it with a clang back in the toolbox. She lifted another. "This one?"

"Pipe wrench."

"There are pipes under there." Hannah dropped the tool but didn't offer another.

"Yes. But right now I'm trying to disconnect the water." Luke sat up, grabbed the tool he needed, and returned to his place under the sink, the chipped tile floor cooling his heated skin.

"That doesn't even look like a crescent."

"It's the brand name of the original maker." Luke loosened the compression fittings from the hot and cold water, then inspected the sink brackets. With any luck, they weren't as rusted as they appeared.

"Maybe I should invent something and name it a Thornton. That'd do a lot to restore the family name in town."

Luke adjusted the tool to one of the rusted bolts. "Thornton is a respected name, and in Heritage any connection is better than no connection. Trust me."

"So, are you staying or fixing this place to sell? I mean, this is the house you grew up in. It's like your family home."

The wrench stilled as a torrent of unwelcome emotions from his past surfaced. He gripped the tool tighter. "Family homes are inherited. I bought this—am buying it. I may have grown up here, but it wasn't my home . . . not really."

"How can you say that? Mrs. Shoemaker was your—"

"Foster mom." He sat up in a quick motion and narrowly missed hitting his head on the sink. "She cared for me in her own way. But I wasn't her son, nor did she want me to be."

"She cared for you, Luke. A lot of people care about you. You just can't see it." Her voice wavered at the end.

People cared about him? Not likely. He leaned back under the sink, found the next bolt, and offered a fair amount of pressure. Nothing.

He had no real roots, no connection to this town. He could disappear and no one would notice. He wasn't even sure God would notice. "A lot of people move out of Heritage, Hannah. Does it really matter if I do?"

"Yes. Because I love . . . this town. And you're an important part." She cleared her throat but her words still came out rough.

"The lumberyard pays the bills, and you know Chet gave me a bargain with this rent-to-own contract. But who knows what'll happen after I finish my degree—if I ever finish."

"You will. This fall will be your final semester, right?"

"Yup." Assuming his last semester grades were good enough. Computer programming had nearly done him in. "And when I'm done, it might be nice to have a newer place." Luke worked on the nut again. *Snap.* Rusted crumbs dropped in his face. He winced. "One with less baggage."

"Not baggage—nostalgia."

He sat up, brushed away the grit, and tossed her the busted nut. "Well, here's a bit of nostalgia for you."

She rubbed her thumb over the rough metal. "What about volunteering at the fire department? If Thomas leaves, they will already be one man down. You can't just walk away. Don't you want to raise your family here?"

She did know how to go to the heart of a matter.

Family. The one thing that had been just out of reach his whole life. Well, as much as he could remember. He'd had a family once, but only a few ghostly memories remained. He pushed away that train of thought and forced a smile. "I believe you're out of questions, but thanks for playing."

Hannah pulled a hand towel off a hook and whipped it at him. "I hate it when you push me away. You push everyone away. The only reason we're friends is because I won't let you shut me out."

"No kidding." A snicker escaped.

"Do you want me to leave?"

Words from their friend Caroline, spoken a few months back, echoed in his head. *If you keep pushing Hannah away, eventually she might actually leave.*

"No." Luke dropped the wrench back in the toolbox with a clang and stood up, brushing his palms against his jeans. "I don't want you to leave."

Hannah stood, dropping her hands on her hips. "Good. Then I'll help. But I'm going to get some water first. Need anything?"

"Water would be great," Luke called as she disappeared around the corner.

If he was going to be working in close proximity to Hannah, he should probably smell a bit fresher. He tugged off his dirt-smudged T-shirt, tossed it toward the laundry room, and reached for a gray one from a basket of clean laundry that he'd left in the hall. Pretty wrinkled but at least it smelled better.

Hannah rounded the corner and stopped, eyes wide, mouth

half open.

He pulled the shirt over his head in one quick motion and tugged it down.

Her gaze snapped to his face and then away. Red crawled up her neck. "Did . . . you want ice?"

"Sure." He leaned down, grabbed another shirt, and tossed it toward her. "Wouldn't want you to ruin that sweater."

Hannah snatched the shirt out of the air and disappeared back the way she'd come, never making eye contact with him. No witty comeback?

Interesting.

Maybe he should have stepped into the laundry room to change his shirt, but they'd been friends for almost twenty years. Perhaps she was modest. Or perhaps—

Luke swallowed and shook away the thought. No good going there. Not yet anyway. Because until he had something to offer, they might as well be back in high school.

Hannah reappeared in record time with two glasses of ice water and wearing his shirt hanging down to her thighs, her long brown hair pulled back in a loose knot/bun thing. Man, she looked cute. He'd managed to keep his feelings for her in a neat little box over the years, but lately that didn't seem enough.

"Are we going to do this sink thing, or what?"

"Right." He followed Hannah into the bathroom. She plopped onto the wooden stool and dug through his toolbox.

"What do you need next? How about this baby?" She lifted up a large monkey wrench and waved it back and forth. The top-heavy wrench crashed into the wall, a chunk of plaster chipping away.

"Don't break my house."

"I'm sorry." Hannah tried to fit the pieces back over the hole.

"Relax. I'm tearing that wall down tomorrow." He lifted his eyebrows at her. "Go ahead, destroy a little more history. I dare you."

Her knuckles whitened on the wrench before she crashed it onto the wall again, sending more plaster crumbs flying.

"Fun, isn't it?"

A smile tugged at her tight lips as she offered one more solid swing. A strange clang echoed from the wall.

His focus darted from Hannah to the crater she'd created. "What was that?"

Hannah dropped the wrench. "I was just swinging at these wooden boards. I swear."

"They're called laths, and they're for the plaster to hold on to, but they shouldn't sound like that." Luke grabbed a small crowbar from his toolbox and wedged it between two of the wooden strips. The splintering of wood split the air as he leaned his weight against the tool. Pushing the pieces aside, he squinted into the dark hole. A black metal box rested in the gap between the studs.

"Now that's history." Hannah's gaze traveled from the box to him then back to the box. "We have to see what's in it."

Luke jabbed the crowbar in another gap to widen the hole, pulled the box free, and examined the lock. It needed an eight-digit code. So much for that. He set the box aside and reached for the wrench.

"You're giving up?"

"Do you know all the junk I've found in these walls? The wall in the upstairs bathroom had hundreds of old razor blades from a slot in the medicine cabinet that was designed to just drop them into the wall. Weird, if you ask me."

"You don't lock trash." Hannah picked up the box and shook it.

"One man's treasure is another man's trash." He pointed to a large bucket that had a growing pile of debris.

"You even want to shut the box out." The words carried a teasing tone, but the frustrated glint in her eye told him this was about a lot more than the box.

Luke dropped the wrench to his toolbox. "Fine, let's try to get it open."

Hannah squeezed his arm. "You won't be sorry."

She was probably right. What trouble could the box cause?

Continue the journey in Heritage with *You belong with Me*

What Secrets Are Hiding Behind the Doors of this Small Town?

I invite you to Heritage, Michigan, a historic small-town with its share of romance and secrets. Let your heart find a home in You Belong with Me, book one in the Restoring Heritage series.

Real estate agent Hannah Thornton loves the historic community of Heritage, Michigan. Unfortunately, selling houses is not one of her fortes. She sees each house and the larger town of Heritage as something to be valued, not sold-off to the highest bidder. When a business mogul arrives in town determined to exploit the land and build a new strip mall, Hannah is determined to stop him from bulldozing her town's past. At first no one supports her efforts—not even her best friend, Luke. Can Hannah help the town of Heritage see that true value lies in the things you cannot put a price tag on?

Even though Luke Johnson has grown up in Heritage as a foster child, he never truly felt like he belonged. Anxious to earn his place in the town and in Hannah's heart, Luke applies for the job of assistant fire chief. But Luke does not anticipate the interview process to unearth secrets from his past he has kept carefully hidden. Will the pain of being honest be worth the risk? Can he pull down the walls he's erected around his bruised heart?

Available where books are sold.
Also available in eBook, autio book, and large print.

Tari Faris has been writing fiction for more than twelve years, and it has been an exciting journey for the math-loving dyslexic girl. She had read less than a handful of novels by the time she graduated from college, and she thought she would end up in the field of science or math. But God had other plans, and she wouldn't trade this journey for anything. As someone told her once, God's plans may not be easy and they may not always make sense, but they are never boring.

Tari has been married to her husband for sixteen wonderful years, and they have three sweet children. In her free time, she loves drinking coffee with friends, rockhounding with her husband and kids, and distracting herself from housework. Visit her at TariFaris.com to learn more about her upcoming books.

Acknowledgments

Thank you to everyone who helped make this book possible.

My Lord and Savior, my parents, Dave and Joyce Thompson, my husband Scott, my children, my WiWee girls (Andrea, Lisa, Alena, Kariss, Tracy, Michelle, and Mandy), My Book Therapy, Beth K. Vogt and so many more who will be fully thanked in You Belong with Me.

A special thanks to Barbara Curtis—you are an amazing editor. Thank you for keeping my character's eyes the same color.

My agent Wendy Lawton who gave me the idea of writing a prequel.

Susan May Warren—helping get it out the door. Your skills and ideas are amazing.

Made in the USA
Lexington, KY
13 November 2019